Alive Nearby

Alive Nearby

BREENA CLARKE

For Najeeb Walid Harb
1974 – 1989

Headstones, Gravestones, Grave Markers
Belonging to a small, private cemetery near Paterson,
New Jersey, these grave markers were loosened and
lost in the Hurricane Irene storm surge and flooding.
A reward is offered for their return.

Contact A. Douglas at amaranthad@gmail.com.

September 20, 2011

Dear M.,

I placed index cards on some supermarket bulletin boards and libraries and at several historical societies along the Passaic River. Damage to the Old Smoot Cemetery is considerable. I was sick on my stomach when I saw it yesterday. I've been told that several grave markers were seen floating away downstream. Mr. Lenny — you know Mr. Leonard Vincent Vander — says he saw some riding away, just floating away. How could they have floated, Mr. Lenny? They are heavy and would have sunk. But that river was angry as hell and it lifted and tore at everything that wasn't bolted down.

We hadn't done much recent maintenance on the old place, in all honesty. I had promised Mr. Lenny I would see that a few things were taken care of, and I didn't follow through. There was always something else that seemed more urgent. Now I'm ashamed to have neglected the old place. And I am ashamed that so much was left on Mr. Lenny.

That river was so angry about being roiled by the hurricane! It disgorged long-buried coffins, slammed them around, cracked some of them, dislodged the grave markers and lifted and carried both caskets and grave markers off. Several have likely washed up into somebody's backyard downstream and the people might not know they ought to find out where they sailed in from. My fear is they may end up as part of a coffee table. Honestly, I think I'd be curious about a stone grave marker with a name carved on it. Some were carved with cherubs. I hope we can retrieve them. How precious they seem now that they're missing.

I've been neglectful of them, and I am supposed to be the conservator. I should have seen that they were cared for. I should have given a care to the caretaker, too. Mr. Lenny is as old as cheese, and I just forgot about him. His niece had to call me to say that he was despondent about the destruction from the storm and could I come up and see about him? It's taken me nearly a month to get up there. My leg ought to be long enough for me to kick myself in the butt. That was always your favorite joke. I know you're shaking with laughter.

I fried chicken, my go to hospitality gift. You remember how wonderfully I pan fry chicken. My car smelled like a picnic at the beach by the time I got up there to see Mr. Lenny. He rallied after a few chicken thighs and some deviled eggs and some very good bourbon. We got caught up, and then we sobbed and discussed the cemetery. He'd had to flee to his niece, Rebecca's place but had returned to his storm-soaked bungalow on the grounds. I promised Rebecca we'd replace the carpet with a new one right away. Seeing the grave markers and some of the caskets floating away had likely shortened Mr. Lenny's life. "It seem like the end of days," he said.

Should I have said a large reward is offered or that the stones are historically significant? I have a list of historical societies in Bergen and Passaic counties, maybe also in

Hudson County. I intend to send letters and flyers to them all. Someone may have already begun making inquiries.

I called the carpet people as soon as I got home.

Love always,
Ma

The unbelievable heartsickness is pushed back for precious moments when she writes the long rambling narrative for her son. M. is alive in the letters. She began the practice at the suggestion of her grief counselor. It does no harm to try to keep him in the world as a wraith at the edge of her consciousness, her grief counselor had said. The idea appealed to her. It seemed a way to add his voice, his presence, back into her days. It comforts her even now, but she would rather no one knew that she's continued the epistolary practice. She doesn't mail them. Of course, that would be veering into troublesome territory, hoping that there was a place to send them, a possibility of an answer.

She'd extracted a promise from him to write letters — to compose snail mail and mail it — if she supported this wholly unexpected "staying off campus with roommates" appeal. All along she'd assumed that he would want to commute to campus, would love the opportunity to have their car to himself. She thought it was more sensible for him to live at home. But he didn't want to. He mentioned going to another university further away. He insisted that he wanted to try living away from home. His voice rose. Her voice rose. After his begging and cajoling, she'd relented. Afterall, everybody wants some freedom, some adventure. Even if they love their parent and are happy at home, they want to leave. They ought to want to leave, it's the age.

In truth she'd twisted his arm. She had wheedled. She'd bargained. If she supported this move, then he must accede to her request. She made him promise solemnly to exchange letters with her, to tell her the daily "goings on" on paper, and she would do the same. They could continue an old family practice. She'd shown him letters from her to her mother when she left home for college. She even pulled out correspondence from their most revered ancestor, Lucille Murtaugh. She was surprised when he agreed. He said he would try. His eyes got juicy then as if he was trying to hold back tears. She was deeply touched. She put stationery and a pen in his backpack.

He did write some letters. They were tentative at first – more filled with questions than information about his day. She'd wanted to know what his classes were like, what he thought about and whom he met. Instead, there were questions in his letter about Beverly and what she was doing and eating. Did Beverly miss him? Tell her that he would be home at the end of the month to play fetch. The tone was disappointingly like a ten-year-old's letter from camp. She could tell he wanted to ask if she missed him and probably, he wanted to say he missed her, too. Perhaps that would seem like giving in, admitting she was right about not leaving home. She knew he missed her. And she felt real sympathy for his confused feeling of longing for home while being glad he'd had the courage to leave it.

His letters are as precious as the old historical correspondence of Lucille Murtaugh and Peter Williams. They are a legacy. She's got them all in a fireproof-waterproof box. Hah! All her letters to M. were lost when his belongings were turned to ash in the fire. All his things that are left are the things that never left with him. She wishes there was a big bag of dirty laundry so she could make a shrine of it, could smell some funky socks, could wipe her face with his underpants.

September 27, 2011

Dear M.,

I love you. I love you and I still find it difficult to live on without you. I am determined to continue, however. I have work to complete.

I love you,
Ma

October 22, 2011

Dear M.,

I have found a wonderful thing. I have found the information I've been looking for. I have discovered the identity of bones we discovered in a cracked coffin amongst the other floaters that we were not able to identify. Lost among the dislodged caskets and driftwood and the interminable mud, he has been identified.

When I saw the pocket watch attached to him, I recognized it. I knew where it had come from, to whom it belonged and why this man should have had it so lovingly placed on his chest. He is inscribed in the Smoot Bible. It states that Bilal was buried in the family yard with a gold watch and "copious tears and gratitude". We've found him! As the flesh has gone back and become part of the ground, it is only his bones and the gold watch that have remained in his dilapidated coffin. Twenty coffins came loose, were battered and broken up and floated off. Yet this one survived. Hurricane Irene brought a huge amount of destruction to the Old Smoot Burial Ground, but spared Bilal's bones, the oldest of the old.

The watch is gold-plated. And though it's inscribed as a gift to Duncan, as in Duncan Smoot, it is not him whose chest it lay upon. Duncan Smoot's grave is still intact on the grounds. The wedding gift that Dossie Smoot inscribed to her husband is the same pocket watch they buried with her father, Papa Bil or Bilal, the man who set young Dossie on the path to her freedom.

If I were a theist, I'd call Bilal a saint. I'd say he was the deity's right-hand person. Ah! He was one of our heroic ancestors, him, and Grandmother Sitton.

His skeleton ought to have been the most fragile of them all for what he'd endured in his life. Because of him an important figure in our line did not spend her life enslaved. He severed his own child from his life to make her free. He started her to freedom and that stunning adventure took her from the docks of Havre DeGrace, Maryland to Russell's Knob, New Jersey.

Of all the bones! His bones were discovered still in the original coffin, mostly undamaged except that the coffin had a large crack in the center of the lid. It struck something. Something struck it. His coffin was excellently constructed, and his body was wrapped with a sachet of herbs that may have further preserved the bones. Others of the very old bones have been discovered to have been in a remarkably well-preserved state, too. Our challenge now is the process of research and reinternment. I want to know exactly what the original internment herbs were and how they were used. I am writing grants and Dr. Campbell is assembling a think tank to help us understand what we must do.

I have ideas.

A full account of how Bil set Dossie on her journey to freedom is included in, "Bolt Toward Freedom: A Young Girl's Account of Her Escape from Bondage to Freedom," by SJS Langer. This is, of course, Sara Jane Smoot Langer,

Dossie Smoot's daughter. Bilal facilitated his daughter's escape. He took her in a small boat from the remote Kenworthy Island plantation owned by Peregrine Kenworthy. It is known and substantiated that Kenworthy operated a punishing agricultural operation growing and harvesting wheat. Though Bilal himself returned to enslavement to cover her escape, he took Dossie up to the port at Havre de Grace, Maryland.

After the war, after the freedom, Duncan Smoot escorted his wife south to find her relatives. They brought their one-year-old infant, Sara Jane, with them and traveled by train to Washington, D.C. In Washington, they hired a wagon to travel to the eastern shore of Maryland, a not unfamiliar area to Duncan Smoot. He had placed an advertisement and received some creditable information that there were still a few remaining people who had been slaves on Kenworthy Island. Peregrine Kenworthy and his family abandoned the place completely when Union troops captured the island and garrisoned troops there. But it was said, some of those who had been enslaved had remained and were living in destitution.

I imagine that Dossie's eyes went wide with terror on that journey south. She'd made her harrowing escape from Kenworthy Island Plantation and had reached safety. Bilal said, "Don't never ever come back," she said in her account of the escape.

Bilal was a sack of bones when they reached Kenworthy Island. He was one of the abandoned ones. Bilal didn't reach Russell's Knob alive. They were caught in an unforgiving rainstorm on the journey through the Octoraro Pass and he caught a croup. According to Sara Jane's account, Bilal's body was dressed, given a casket, and buried in the Russell's Knob cemetery with a gold watch on his chest.

Love,
Ma

October 30, 2011

Dear M.,

Good news. There will soon be extensive testing and research on Bilal's bones. We've received a grant to undertake it. I get a little tearful to think of scraping and daubing and whittling them away. Silly. Bil would probably be quite happy to have his bones tell us something. I'm sure the old one would think it was fitting.

I don't know if I can explain how I felt when I first perused Bilal's bones. Imagine! They've lain below ground so long, and we are connected to them directly, though zig-zaggedly, through our lineage. Bilal is Dossie Smoot's father and she's the wife of Duncan Smoot, the brother of our direct ancestor, Harriet Smoot Wilhelm Murtaugh. By the standards of the clannish folks of Russell's Knob, I can be said to be Bilal's daughter descended. Perhaps if Bilal had not sent his little daughter away to freedom, my entire line would not have lived. Dossie's arrival in Russell's Knob changed the lives of the Smoot family including my great, great great grandmother. I wanted to kiss the bones, to genuflect before them or burn some incense. Not knowing why, I did burn some sage. *Dem bones, dem dry bones. Dem bones, dem dry bones.* Daughter connected to her mama and her mama and her mama all the way to Bilal's little girl put aboard a shallop on the eastern shore of Maryland in 1849.

I want to cry for joy to consider our ancestors knew all along, in some mysterious, atavistic, deeply intuitive way that bones could talk and needed to talk and that one day we'd be able to hear what they'd say.

I want Bilal's bones to indict America for the transgressions, the great sins of our national past. Perhaps beloved Bilal will only want us to remember his courage, his resilience, his patience, and we'll discover his wishes in his bones.

I'm impatient. We've been too patient. I've always believed that change would come. And here it is: Bilal has taught me something. Patience. What goes around comes around.

Beloved Bilal was considered nothing more than a commodity. His life was viciously painful I know that. What evidence we have confirms that the Kenworthy Plantation on Kenworthy Island, which is now an army proving ground, was a cruelly administered agricultural operation. This is where our beloved ancestor Dossie Smoot was born, and this was the place from which Bilal, who never expected to see her again, removed her to set her to freedom.

I cannot begin to fathom those feelings, those feelings that came at dawn of the day after he sent her away. Though perhaps I do know something about the loss of a child. How could he bear it? And now I know Bilal will have the last word on Kenworthy Plantation. I can't help feeling triumphant for him and the descendants of people from Kenworthy. I wouldn't "help it" if I could. We have triumphed. Bilal's story will inform what is known about the lives of enslaved people and what they endured to create the agricultural legacy of the Mid-Atlantic. Peregrine Kenworthy was a self-made monster, a trader of slaves who went into plantation agriculture to grow wheat. I refuse to give him and his spawn the honor of sharing responsibility for anything. They deserve only the shame of having enslaved Bilal and Dossie and Dossie's mother and all the others who lived and perished at Kenworthy.

What would we say about Bilal if we had ever seen his flesh upon these bones? What were his physical dimensions? We'll know that soon.

I have closed my eyes and imagined him. I like the heroic picture in my mind. I see tall and broad and wide-faced and like a Hollywood actor. I accept that he was likely much more scarred, bent, deformed by infirmities, and smaller in stature than I imagine. He must have been a muscled knot of a man to have endured actual torture and privation and still lived to be very old. How old was he? The analysis of the remains will answer this question. My imagination is, I confess, constrained by what I have seen in my lifetime, and I think it may not be multifarious enough for Bilal's story.

M., you have no doubt met Bilal by now. My vision of that place where you are and I am not is very specific to me. I see you in a large comfortable room with food and fire and beguiling aromas and plenty of light and the pleasure and feelings of happiness and love and understanding — deep, deep understanding. Understanding being the hallmark of the place. It is a very specific place. Everything is copacetic there, M., everything is everything somehow. Bilal is there. He's a saint. And you are there because you are certainly a saint taken too soon. Have you embraced Bilal by this time?

Would you bring him to me in a dream? I would like to see his face. It would be a secret between us. I would tell no one. They would think I'd gone around the bend.

I wish the technicians wouldn't touch his bones too much performing tests that will diminish them in any way. Perhaps that just isn't possible.

Love,

Ma

(I love to sign off as Ma because you said it that way. You called me this. I write it, and I hear it, and I can recall the exact intonation in my head. I write to see it, hear it and to remember my sweet baby's voice.)

October 31, 2011

Dearest Malcolm,

When I write M., I think of Malcolm, what it stands for. Then I recollect you. I see a picture of you, and I smile from inside. I feel better briefly. I ought to fill a page with your name. Malcolm. Malcolm, Malcolm. I'm afraid my head would spin so much I could not stand. Malcolm — oh, how I wish I were yelling this name out loud — screaming it louder than loud! Malcolm!

Halloween: Our most confusing and most pagan holiday. Children tearing through the streets demanding candy. I recall the year you were seven or eight when you wore a creepy skull mask and a suit that was an exposed skeleton. When you saw yourself in the mirror, I could tell you didn't like the look. I didn't either. Perhaps you had frightened yourself and the charm of Halloween was broken. That was the last year you wore a "kid's" costume. Masks only after that year. Tomorrow and the next day we'll celebrate All Saints Day and the Day of the Dead. I embrace these now. These are truly my holidays. You are my saint, and every day is the Day of the Dead.

Ma

November 25, 2011

Dear M.,

Because Mr. Lenny insisted that I come, I went to Thanksgiving dinner yesterday at Rebecca Vander Jackson's house. Mr. Lenny must have sensed that we all needed a family dinner after the last few months. Hurricanes get over, blow through, but they leave a lot of debris and they take a fair amount away. We are still reeling from the destruction to the cemetery. It's sensitive, M., the disposition of remains. It matters what you do.

In honor of all factions of our outsider community, I made two pies: one sweet potato and one pumpkin. And since Rebecca added whipped cream to all the slices, no one could tell the difference.

Love,
Ma

January 9, 2012

Dearest M.,

I'm thankful the holidays are over. Christmas and New Year's are troublesome. The conclusion of this past year brought about the conclusion of a major phase of my life.

We've officially closed The Williams-Murtaugh Institute. It became official on December 31, 2011. Enrollment slipped very dramatically in the past five years, as you know, to a level that does not allow us to operate the bricks-and-mortar institution as we have always done. We were the institution of opportunity for Black women when there were no others who would see to our best interests and our education. I hesitate to say we are no longer needed. We are needed differently. We are preserving the legacy. It has fallen to me to steward the end of the Institute as a school of higher learning and into a research institute and museum of the culture of African Americans with special emphasis on the Mid-Atlantic region.

I have a peculiar sort of news to begin this new year. It is human nature to reckon time. We are always adding up the minutes. I often whine about the minutes until I can be with you. Even I can see this as self-pity. But I do pity myself for not having you. Despite being a scholar and a historian, I still . . . long. What else can I do? Well, finish the archiving, finish the histories.

We've been working diligently, if slowly, deliberately. I've discovered something not previously accounted for. The papers of Dr. Ismail Murtaugh, physician, were collected and archived by Lucille Murtaugh, his daughter and one of the founders of the Institute and were arranged into several groups by my mother, Dr. Barbara Elaine Madison. Dr. Murtaugh's correspondence and the diaries of his experiences as a soldier in the United States Colored Troops are collected in the biographical text "To Serve Where I Am Needed, The Civil War Recollections of Ismail Murtaugh, M.D.," written and published by his daughter.

There are other texts and some medical drawings as well. When I began a full shelf read of the volumes in our library collections, I discovered ass previously unknown text by Dr. Murtaugh. I admit that I have been proceeding with no haste at all. I have indulged in the pleasure of reading these fascinating texts. It is so restful and personally fulfilling to sit and read, to have the job of your dreams, the job of caring for, preserving, reveling in the beautiful and important books that are my legacy. There are books and ephemera in the thousands. And I am counting them all for the first time.

I have lollygagged, makes me smile remembering you loved this expression and would stick a finger in your mouth and waggle your head whenever I said it.

I've inherited our ancestors' work, and I am glad. Maybe I was reluctant at first. But there is much to do since the flood and there have been several very significant discoveries. I am not hurrying through the library.

We've discovered some surprising things in the boxes and file cabinets and crates and folders. We are Dr. Brynne

Campbell and me. As of the New Year, Dr. Campbell, hired by the Institute to direct the archiving and cataloging of the Institute's records, is reviewing documents, books, and ephemera. She first came to the Institute's archives in pursuit of information on Black-identified, autonomous settlements in New Jersey for her Ph.D. thesis on African Americans in the Garden State. Everything about our town, Russell's Knob, surprised her. She's become enchanted with the town's existence, its history and the preservation of its documents and books. Our mountain of documents and our collections are intoxicating to her. I'm pleased to have her assistance and her considerable scholarship.

Something very unsettling has been found at bottom of a file cabinet of no particular importance from the outside. It is not labeled in any way. How puzzling! It is a simple wooden file with a pencil drawer, a file drawer, and a deep file drawer. The deep portion contained a plastic-wrapped bundle. I put on my gloves and ran my fingers over the plastic bubble wrap. Concluding that its plastic wrap meant nothing, I cut it away and it popped and farted merrily in the way of bubble wrap. This bundle had been wrapped and hidden recently for sure. Beneath the plastic lay a leather-bound volume, some pages attached to the binding and some not. I pulled my mask over my nose and mouth in anticipation of some wonderful find heretofore unknown. I was cautious though. It is never a good idea to open these old boxes and folders and envelopes without guarding against airborne dust.

I turned the leather folder face down, opened it at the back, and peeled back the loose pages. At the back of the book were drawings of, in very great, horrifying detail, what appear to be horror-movie-like medical operations. The air went out of me at the first sight of them and the accompanying text. I sat alone in the attic room with this book and lost my breath for a while. I vomited though I am used to looking at early medical drawings that can be very graphic.

Could our beloved Dr. Murtaugh have performed these operations?

When I calmed myself, I turned the book over and began to read from the beginning of the text. The handwriting was recognizable as Dr. Ismail Murtaugh's, Lucille's father.

Dr. Murtaugh wrote:

Her words to me were these when I asked her how she came to be so disfigured. "I been used this way since I was a baby," she said flatly. By that I believe she meant that she had been a victim of torture since her early childhood. Many, many were her healed scars. She was unmoved by my expression of concern and sympathy. Horrified, incredulous, concern. She resented my look of pity though. That made her look at me so dully. I was shocked and appalled at what had been done to her at the hands of the butchering Dr. P. She named him. Why would she not? He could not deal out any more to her than he had already inflicted. I felt such revulsion and pity. I recognized the work of a trained medical man. And though I would describe her treatment as butchery, no butcher would do the things perpetrated upon this woman. There were healed scars, carbuncles, hematoma of every sort, tissues taken away and added. He was a doctor, not a butcher, trained or otherwise.

She came to me through word of mouth from some other women that I had been gentle with, that I had helped with their womanly worries in the camp.

It can be said that his medical experiments, conducted without anesthesia and without the consent of the patient, reveal that Dr. P. suffered from a sexual perversion and what is now referred to as a sadistic nature after the well-known Marquis de Sade.

Whose comment is this? The script does not match Gree-Gree's hand precisely. Can it be Dr. Murtaugh's comment? The ink differs from other parts of the text though that is not necessarily conclusive evidence that he did not write this on another occasion than the rest - used a different pen, had a different pot of ink.

Who is this Dr. P.? The journal does not say. It describes some bits of his whereabouts and his reputation — accounts by the victims of his butchery. It appears that Dr. Murtaugh circulated among several contraband camps to investigate these disturbing acts by interviewing women who had been "treated" by Dr. P. Dr. He noted that this man did present his work as scientific findings relevant to the field of women's childbearing health. Is it that Dr. Murtaugh did not furnish the man's name somewhere in his work because it was well known at the time and could have been guessed. The possibility of censure or indictment of this man for what was done to slave women by him could never have been accomplished in that era. Knowing what we know now I'd guess Dr. Murtaugh himself would have been accused and censured.

I read the whole document. It is sixty or so pages in Dr. Murtaugh's hand. Some words were difficult to distinguish. I will have to return to the text to decipher those passages that I could not understand on the first pass. I won't be able to face it right away. I felt fortunate that Dr. Campbell was away at a conference and didn't call until very late in the evening. I was still in the attic office with the new discovery. She apologized for calling late and for waking me and added that she'd gone for a drink with the other panelists. I'm afraid I must have come across as peeved. I could hear my voice sounding falsely cheerful. She was a bit stiff when she said goodnight and hung up. I offered no excuse for my mood.

I feel sorry that Dr. Campbell will wake up thinking I'm annoyed that she went to this conference and is hanging out with her colleagues and friends. She will think that is what caused me to seem a little cool. But it was that journal.

Really, I don't want her to see it. Foolish, I know. She's grown. She's a scholar who has written about horrors and witnessed some, I am so sorry to say. But you can't care about someone and ever want them to have these pictures seared in their brain. And the images will be seared. Unbelievable shock at the horrors that some human beings are capable of inflicting and that some humans have been able to endure.

I feel I must return to Dr. Murtaugh's journal, to the one that lays out the gruesome story. The paper is the same or similar to the paper in his other texts and the ink is consistent with his other writings. Of course, these documents were read by Gree-Gree. In her own papers Gree-Gree refers to materials that were considered inappropriate for the delicate constitutions of young women. Are these the papers she was referring to? She mentions having removed some text from the complete manuscript of Dr. Murtaugh's that she published after her father died. Removed. Hidden, but not destroyed. Gree-Gree was a better scholar than me. I would have burned these drawings and papers.

I returned to my attic desk after I'd showered, dressed, checked email, and fixed a pot of coffee. The coffee slowed me. I had been rushing through the steps of my ablutions and the coffee eased me back into myself. The blessed contradiction of a cup of coffee: It'll give you a charge of energy, but can make you mellow and ruminative as well. Coffee helps me ease down into my best head, my thinking head.

I decided to begin by examining the leather sleeve then the papers that filled it. The sleeve was several shades of brown though it must have started out as one shade of thick, brown leather. The sleeve was embossed with a design that I'd seen before in Dr. Murtaugh's possessions. In fact, I recognized this leather folder as part of a gift set given to Dr. Murtaugh by his devoted friend, Petrus Wilhelm, a.k.a. Peter Williams. There is a diary in the set that continues some of Dr. Murtaugh's chronological records, so it is stored with the chronological collection of diaries. And I have come across a smaller, rectangular pouch, smelling of tobacco and darker with wear than the other two items. Should these items be displayed together so that we can highlight an example of men's leather goods of the fin de siecle period? That will be a decision for Dr. Campbell. I am perfectly confident that Brynne will be named as curator of the Museums of the Williams-Murtaugh Institute at our upcoming board meeting. She is qualified of course, and she is passionate. I am nominating her and will give her my full endorsement. It is fait accompli.

Peter Williams, calling on the leather goods emporium in Newark, chose this superb three-piece professional man's set for his dear friend's birthday. The pouch bears an embossed name that we have found on a commercial map that shows their storefront on Halsey Street in Newark. It would have been an expensive present. Williams was devoted to Ismail Murtaugh, the man who saved his life. I wonder why Dr. Murtaugh used this folder, a generous gift from his friend, to hide a manuscript he wanted no one to see. Aha! It's obvious he didn't put it in the sleeve. Gree-Gree did that. Perhaps. Don't jump to conclusions, right? Another hand may be in this. In fact, any one of three or four sets of hands could have changed the destiny of this document. The fascination is that it has all come this far.

Yes, I'll listen to my ancestors' advice about being too quick to decide a thing. Consciously or sub-consciously Gree-Gree must have thought that something so sensitive must be put inside something whose tough leather exterior could conceal it. Or perhaps she thought that eventually its contents would be examined, that it wouldn't be simply tossed away because it is so obviously an important item? No one has admitted to looking inside this folder, but no one ever burned it. I can guess who put bubble wrap around it. It wasn't hidden so much as secreted. Dr. Barbara Elaine

Madison knew I would find this bundle. Who else but my mother?

Musing and drinking coffee and not opening the folder for several hours, I was jolted from my reverie by my phone. I glanced at it guiltily, seeing Dr. Campbell's. Why? If I'd told Brynne last night about what I'd discovered, she wouldn't have had a night's rest. I just said, "Come to the attic office." The stuff I've read has left me without any social lacquer.

As I fixed coffee for Brynne, she looked at me in complete puzzlement. I didn't explain except to say that there was something very important I'd discovered in an old leather folder belonging to Dr. Murtaugh that together we should decide what to do with.

M., you always admired Dr. Murtaugh. He was painted very large in your eyes, a heroic figure. I've often dreamed of his Civil War exploits as the inspiration for a great film, a sort of, *Glory,* told from the perspective of a Black soldier.

Dr. Ismail Murtaugh was what Russell's Knob needed after the Civil War. He had trained before the war at the American Eclectic College in Chicago. Obstetrics was a particularly urgent area since the last practicing midwife left Russell's Knob to go to St. Louis in 1868. Dr. Murtaugh became known for his gentleness with female patients. He had an abundance of respect and compassion and for them and took genuine joy in bringing children into the world. His war experiences obviously impressed on him a deep respect for pain and suffering and a delight in babies and children.

Harriet Smoot Wilhelm was mature when she married Ismail Murtaugh after the war so Lucille was thought to be a miracle baby and a truly fortunate daughter. Her father was well respected and loved and he was devoted to her and her mother. However, facts do appear to suggest that Dr. Murtaugh was also quite fond of Sally Vander and is likely the father of her son, Marcus. Nothing much is known about Marcus Vander. He is in our database as someone we want to know more about. As you see, we have a biological connection to the Vanders.

I told Brynne to do as I'd done. Just read. I laid out a pair of gloves and a dust mask for her. I put the document on the desk and left the room saying, "In the kitchen when you're done."

My next thought was to drink down a large glass of merlot and get loopy-headed and wait for her to come downstairs. My second thought was to fix a pot of potato leek soup and warm the kitchen with steamy, fragrant home cooking. I decided to do both things.

Potato leek is my chicken soup. I believe in the medicinal value of potatoes and leeks, a couple of rough, earthy, common foodstuffs made blissful with the addition of cream and butter blended smooth and thick in defiance of hunger and poverty and illness. My recipe is based on Gree-Gree's of course. For modern tastes the amount of cream is moderated. In her original version, in the treatment of all respiratory complications, Lucille Murtaugh recommended that the soup be made immediately after the cow had been milked and the cow's hair scraped from it. The still-frothy milk gets added to the simmering leeks and butter, real, real butter in Gree-Gree's case, a lot of it. Salt is added. Lucille's compendium of home-based treatments of illness also included the suggestion that large amounts of cayenne pepper can be added to the soup in cases to address catarrh. Her potato leek soup was most often served in the morning as the breakfast meal for someone needing comfort. I wanted to have a good meal prepared for Brynne when she'd finished reading. I figured she might feel a little nauseous.

I nursed that soup and it was wonderfully smooth. This smoothness is the important part and can so easily not go well. There can be separation of the oily butter and the delicate yet heavy cream, half& half is better. The soup is ruined if there are globules floating on top. But you lose the potato chunk texture if you use a blender. Properly lowering the heat and gently stirring the room-temp dairy into the mix is the technique. It takes concentration, time to ruminate on what is troubling the chest or stomach of the loved one.

I made biscuits, too.

At about 5 p.m. I went up to the attic to fetch Brynne. She'd been up there all day and hadn't made a peep of noise. I began to worry. She jumped from startle when she heard me call her name. It looked as though she'd fallen asleep after her crying. Her face had creases.

I touched her shoulder very lightly. She tore off her gloves and flung them against the wall, saying, "Oh my goodness." I reached up, pulled the dust mask tangled in her hair off, and threw it against the wall, too.

Though I would have done anything to keep this awful account of the atrocities of Dr. P. from her, I am glad that she read it. I gathered up the document and drawings and shoved them back where they'd been. I was rough with them. I was suddenly very angry that these godawful words and pictures on something as fragile and as impermanent as paper and ink had not faded. The ink was dark and solid and black, and the paper was not even very yellowed.

Brynne ate a large bowl of soup quickly, ate a biscuit in two- and- a half bites, then had another bowl of my soup before saying anything. When she stopped eating Brynne started squishing her semi-voluminous retro Afro. Her hair was harmonious, but disorderly; unrestrained, but well-groomed. She had a well moisturized, rounded head of hair. A dedicated moisturizer, she's given herself alternate rituals to reclaim herself from childhood hair grooming nightmares. She's told me a few things and they are not happy stories. I understand she is thinking deeply when she mashes and squishes her hair with both hands.

Did Lucille Murtaugh hide these documents? Were they concealed or just misplaced, unaccounted for, lost? Is there any mention of this document in any other document in our collection? Yes, Lucille Murtaugh records that some very explicit medical material was removed from her father's journals and diaries and that texts for use at the Institute were carefully edited so that "Father's most graphic and intimate notations were not included for being too sensitive for the minds of laypersons." I'd done a bit of hunting through Gree-Gree's diaries. What if anything had she said about these documents?

The hiding. The secrecy. These things are a way of life for people of Russell's Knob. Funny though that people so full of secrets would keep such complete and copious records.

When I can consider these papers and drawings calmly, with my usual scholarly eye, will I see their historical significance or simply be nauseated? I worry that my squeamishness will cause me to decide to shove them back in a drawer. I hope Brynne won't let me.

The documents are proof that this Dr. P. did experiment on enslaved women. No possible consent could be given. Here is documentation that these experiments were performed without any anesthesia other than alcohol by mouth and that the experiments took the form of sadistic torture. So much of modern gynecology is based upon these horrible acts. What is Dr. Murtaugh's part in it? Brynne is satisfied, as am I, that Dr. Murtaugh recorded this evidence well after the events and his account is based on the testimony of its victims. He undertook to make the drawings to have a record of the atrocities. It is a superb work of translation and transcription: the words to graphic drawing. Perhaps he felt his words would be inadequate. The drawings are so graphic it hurts my eyes to look at them. I am separating them from the text and have placed each sheet in a document folder and placed them in a box that ought to have a warning sticker on it. I'll just write: SENSITIVE. This box will go back onto the shelf with Dr. Murtaugh's things.

What must Gree-Gree have thought of these drawings? A woman of her era? Well now who is to say that Gree-Gree could not have handled seeing them? Would she have lost her lunch? She comes across these many decades through her diaries as an enormously tough, enterprising, intellectually rigorous woman.

Love,
Ma

January 12, 2012

Dear M.,

You know I like root vegetables in autumn and winter. Eating them makes me feel right-minded and purposeful, because it makes such good sense to eat hearty and husky and earthy food when it's cold and mushy and desperate outside. Why desperate, M.? I just feel sort of like a criminal on the run since we found that tough stuff, those pernicious drawings. I don't know what to call them and I don't know how to feel about it. I only know that I ought to self-medicate with hearty, tasty things. I must be reminded that Dr. Murtaugh helped people to survive, and he created my family and that I had better just hold on and keep steady and do what must be done.

Brynne shrieked that my kitchen smelled like a box of farts. "What are you cooking?" she asked, mashing her nose. "Smells like cabbage."

It was rutabaga, not cabbage. It amused me that she didn't know the difference and that she didn't like the aroma. One of the most comforting things in winter is to enter a house with the robust aromas of root vegetable cooking down to softness, sweet potatoes or yams, that can cook low all day and are marvelous with butter; cabbage boiling gently; and the yellow turnip, the rutabaga going great guns in a microwave until soft enough to mash up with butter and bacon fat and salt. This is winter kitchen bliss.

Perhaps she is right that these gassy, earthy things do smell up the place. Maybe I'm holding onto them in defiance of the smell of sushi, which I don't like at all not being fond of raw flesh in cuisine. Brynne likes sushi rather a lot and that surprised me some, which miffed her a little. Root veggies remind me of my mother and her mother and her mother and Gree-Gree. Perhaps they remind her of something else. Do you remember the stuffed toy you called Rudy Bagas? That was my idea, of course, but you always chuckled when you said it. It was a big, lumpy, bear-looking sort of plush toy that you would hug or pummel.

Love,
Ma

January 19, 2012

Dear M.,

I'm sad and sorrowful without you. But I have not gone silly, stupid. I know that I'm not telling you anything you don't know, if things are the way I think they must be in the afterlife. I hope for a verdant glade, mountain vista, sparkling turquoise beach, field of sunflowers, mother's fried chicken, a roasted sweet potato, butter-slathered biscuits, and butter pecan ice-cream with no calories. No sirens, lights, screams, guns, and no policemen interfering with the peaceful embrace of my wildest dreams. You are aware and still care about me. Though this isn't altogether plausible, I know you are close by, and that is all of it.

Ma

January 21, 2012

Dearest M.,

We have decided the pernicious material should be made available to scholars. We are going to be stingy with them though. Access only to the serious and vetted. I'm working on a letter to The American College of Obstetricians and Gynecologists about the material. As they've begun to recognize the contributions of enslaved women whose victimization at the hands of torturers led to advances in medical equipment and procedures in obstetrics, they will want to view these documents.

Though it makes no sense to say it, I'm glad you aren't here to see these drawings. But since I imagine you as peering over my shoulder in my every day, how can you not see them? I realize it's that I'm glad I don't have to see you see the drawings, the cruelties. I'm still exercising my maternal thing. Are you still my child? Remember the time I covered your eyes so you wouldn't see the deranged guy shitting in a trashcan on the corner of 51st and Ninth Avenue in The City? You went purple with annoyance. Even a disgusting memory is blissful sometimes.

No matter the relationship, I love you still,
Ma

January 26, 2012

Dear M.,

Dr. Campbell and I have put the disturbing drawings and materials aside for the past week. I sent my letter to the American College of Obstetricians and Gynecologists. What response do I expect? I expect a response. It is well documented and most medical historians acknowledge that the father of modern gynecology, Dr. J. Marion Sims, conducted experiments on enslaved women. Perhaps they will know to whom Dr. Murtaugh has referred as Dr. P. As distasteful as these documents are, they are important for us to understand what horrors were perpetrated on enslaved women.

I am concerned about taking care of Brynne, too. She's faced these papers and drawings bravely, but I'm aware of how they might affect her. They are apt to be triggers. I feel privileged at times like this that I was so well cared for as a youngster. My body was not violated. I was supported and loved unconditionally, and I've come to understand that was a great bit of luck. I can't take it for granted.

I consider myself to have been a good mother, a good parent. I provided, and I loved. You were easy. Brynne has been extremely courageous. She literally raised and educated herself. I'm glad she's here. She belongs to Russell's Knob. What say?

Your Ma

February 1, 2012

Dear Malcolm,

Okay, okay. I will not say it. I will not say that every month is Black History Month. Here we are at another Black History Month. As it happens, Dr. Campbell and I are both busy this month. We have two conferences to attend. We're proceeding slowly with the new documents. I am concerned that they are handled carefully. Those drawings make my skin uncomfortable, something between itching, burning and being scraped. I'm paranoid about them getting uploaded to the internet. I don't want some creep seeing them and getting off.

Love,
Ma

February 28, 2012

Dear M.,

Happy Birthday to me! Was that you I was looking for last night? I had that dream again, the one where I'm pursuing someone through a series of strangely shaped and illogical rooms. This dream has become so familiar that I recognize it right away for what it is. Most of the time I can wake up, but last night I couldn't. I couldn't catch up with you, and I couldn't come awake. But don't leave me. Don't stop being around.

Fifty-three is just a number. It means little when weighed against the brevity of your life.

Ma

March 1, 2012

Dear M.,

Did you know? Did I say it before? I considered calling you Martin or Marcus. You know me. If there was any special magic in assigning a name, I wanted yours to be intellectually rigorous and bold and unflinching. I never considered Fred or Tyrone or Tavon. So, I decided on Malcolm, a heroic name. I could have called you Hannibal and I can imagine your face at that suggestion. It's a great name – heroic, mellifluous, different. Ha. Ha. What things would I do differently? None. Except perhaps I would have . . . I don't know what different I could have done.

We are hard at work on the history and other projects connected to the collection.

Always thinking of you,
Ma

March 24, 2012

Dear M.,

I flatter myself when I say I want to change the way readers remember American history. But, quite simply, this is what I want to do.

Confidence at last. I can take my own temperature. Finally, with respect for my own accomplishments and respect, too, for my longevity, I feel capable of carrying forward with the work. However, I am entertaining some problems for the first time. I realize that I now depend upon your presence in my head. The work requires another interrogator. You've been patient enough to listen to my thoughts. Beloved interlocutor, without you I hardly have any voice at all in my mind, but my own. Seems hollow.

I miss you. You are gone and, though your presence persists and pervades my day to day, it doesn't always give me comfort. I miss you keenly in my body, and my body can't help reacting tearfully when it twinges with feelings. I simply can't work very much when I cry at every turn. So now I'm imploring the ancestors to let you sit with them crowned and glorified during the day, so you'll not regale me with daydreams of our life together. It was too lovely and now it makes me break down crying to remember it. Often, I float away on beautiful recollections of our life and waste valuable time.

M., ignore the previous. Who else knows me and who
else loves The People as I do? Please do not ever leave my
thoughts. This is official: Day or night, I want always to be
haunted by you, to remember.

Love,
Ma

March 25, 2012

Dearest M.,

Am I calling you? My mind wanders to your side. I was troubled all night by so much dreaming about you. I dreamt of what you said about this and that and the other. Were you trying to show me Bilal? I felt myself to be following you. But my mind became filled with a panic I could not identify. I felt my feet sinking into quicksand and being unable to rescue a drowning kitten. I could not see Bilal's face or yours last night.

Return to my dreams,
Ma

March 26, 2012

M.,

Only your voice reached me last night. I chased you from one room to another attempting to locate you. I have never liked hide-and-seek games. Please quiet down. I woke with my heart in my throat and my chest throbbing. I felt as though I'd received a blow. Yes, yes, you were never wrong.

The upshot: Nothing is new under the sun, and nothing is old either. Living well is the best revenge. Every goodbye ain't gone. Every shut eye ain't sleep (don't I know this!) What goes around comes around. That's a perennial favorite and I think of it often, though it makes me dizzy to contemplate it. I realize you were trying to comfort me. If you fill my head with these old sayings, then I will have a sense of certainty, know that life "is what it is."

I've completed a draft of *Maroon New Jersey: The Complete History of Russell's Knob*. I am simply putting our lives in the record. Those who are interested in the text will find it and appreciate it for what it is, a record.

I've begun to feel differently now that you're gone, M. Of course, in the larger, overarching manner of grief I am changed. But in small ways, too. Now I wish I could leave a more personal picture of the people of Russell's Knob, something more than just the record, something that erases their invisibility and yours and replaces it with the sights and smells and hungers. I want to record everything about them and you, their thoughts, their dreams, your thoughts and dreams. To erase invisibility? That's a lofty aim. I want to replace the nothing that is known of our ancestors with the much they preserved of themselves with bits of extra that will make them very real to a reader.

They - White Americans - think we have no ancestors or that we don't know anything about them. When some Whites ask why we seek to keep unearthing the past, I say that I will forget when they do. When they forget that they are someone I am not and the advantage is in their favor, I will forget. I am very prickly on this.

Dr. Campbell and I worked together on an updated mission statement for our website.

> We are founded upon bedrock. We are dedicated
> to the education, development, and well-being of
> Women of the African Diaspora. We are committed
> to researching, restoring lost history, and preserving
> the legacy of our community for the 21st century.
> The Williams-Murtaugh Institute was founded
> in 1908 with the assets of the estate of Peter
> Williams, aka, Petrus Wilhelm, resident of Russell's
> Knob, New Jersey, the owner of the Peter Williams
> Brewery.

It was her idea that we ought to include all women of African ancestry regardless of so-called national boundaries.

Malcolm, am I simply trying to relive a past that has passed? Possibly. Although I am not so foolish with grief and loss that I think this is possible. The People of Russell's Knob are gone by and large. Except for me. Except for the one or two of us who are left of their line. However, I insist that our true legacy is not through our biological connections, but our interconnectedness of spirit, our relationship to our tangible history and the importance of having, against all odds, preserved our legacy.

The people of Russell's Knob were once quite a grand settlement. Russell's Knob was a successful mixed-race community. We were a blended soup for many generations. Of course, this vast array was just a rumor until after the Civil War when Ismail Murtaugh and his photography obsession came to Russell's Knob. The evidence is there in family photos. Blue Blacks, cinnamon-coloreds, red-bones, tans, butter-coloreds, swarthy Whites, and pale Whites. There are African wooly heads and European silkies and curly ginger-heads in these photographs. All the diverse appearances occur in all the large families in Russell's Knob.

The papers of Lucille Murtaugh - her journals, diaries, and compendiums, and her collections and catalogues - have formed the substance of my research. I added additional documentary material to what is already there by her hand and superb brain. She was an unacknowledged genius. If she were a White man of her day, she'd have run the world. I believe the depth of her wisdom and the all-encompassing compassion that were essential to her nature would have made her an excellent world leader if the field had been fair. She could have stood beside John J. Astor and Andrew

Carnegie; Theodore Roosevelt, Woodrow Wilson, J. Edgar Hoover; and Albert Einstein, and Ludwig Wittgenstein. She would easily have been better than any of these at combining creative imagination, leadership, scholarship, and intellectual rigor with compassion.

Maybe I am exaggerating, M., because I love her so much and because I believe I understand her deeply because I have read her journals and diaries and because I've lived all of my life with the objects she preserved. They are a huge mound of belongings that we are only now beginning to bring into their best future and their own best placement so that they are available to scholars and regular people. My head rings with pithy phrases about the urgency of documenting and preserving her work.

I've chosen to call Lucille Murtaugh my Gree-Gree, my great-great grandmother, the mother of my mother's grandmother's mother-in-law and before her back to the next which is why. Gree-Gree, greatest of the great I suppose. You know I've called her that since I first read her journals the summer between high school and college. And because of those journals I became hooked on archiving and preserving. Poor angry, Robert Murtaugh, Lucille's son tried to destroy the vital familial link by ordering his wife to burn the entire collection of journals after his mother's death. She did not. The journals were rescued and preserved by Pearl Miller Murtaugh and passed to her daughter, Lillian and to her daughter, Barbara, then to me, her daughter Amarantha. When I feel I must give myself a heroic purpose, I pledge myself to follow in this tradition.

Malcolm, I would not sound so feverish and self-important if it were not for grieving your loss.

"All items on paper are impermanent ultimately, Dr. Douglas," our new curator said. I was stung to hear this. The women of my line have done so much to preserve these papers that it sounded like all their efforts were futile. But I knew how right she was. What would happen if there were a fire?

"Well, yes, Dr. Campbell," I replied with a smile. "Paper is vulnerable."

"Digitizing the collection will give scholars access and ordinary people access to the history. Look at what happened in Georgetown at the library. Priceless artifacts on paper from the Federalist period were turned to ashes because of inept workers and a fast-moving fire."

Her face froze in shock at her own words. Certainly, someone had told her about your death. She's a kind, compassionate, caring person, but the words had just tumbled out of her mouth. My eyes forgave her, reassured her.

Then she said, "Dr. Douglas, can we keep the project confidential for a while? I want to be the first to archive the photos and digitize them and write a narrative for a book. They would make a stunning collection of photographic images of a once autonomous African American community. Russell's Knob is that rare, undiscovered place, a place that some of us Black people have only dreamed of, have longed for. It's that place where being Black was the same as being smart and strong and courageous and it's a place few other African Americans have been to or even know about. Please don't be selfish with the photos, Amy."

I jumped a bit, I suppose, because she instantly reacted

with a different face. Her expression changed from something on the order of sweet and seductive to embarrassed. I can't say how I appeared to her. She surprised me when she used my first name. I had asked her to call me Amy, and she'd insisted on keeping with Dr. Douglas. Dr. Douglas. Dr. Douglas. The sudden switch in her moment of trying to charm her way into using my heirlooms feels calculated. The project is her idea to publish a coffee table book of photographs of our town. She wants me to give approval for her book. I will, of course, and, of course, once I recovered from the shock of hearing my first name coming out of her mouth, I was pleased.

I was stunned that she used the term "selfish," M. I never think of myself as acting selfishly, but what else am I doing by keeping the photographs only accessible to a small group of scholars? Why not digitize and publish them so they can be seen by all people?

We have early photographs of Duncan Smoot and Dossie Smoot and their daughter, Sarah Jane Smoot Langer; Harriet Smoot Wilhelm Murtaugh; Dr. Ismail Murtaugh and, because Dr. Murtaugh was a talented amateur photographer, there are not only many photographs of his daughter, my Gree-Gree, Lucille Murtaugh, but also Mary Wilhelm/Williams and Analiese Brown/Williams, the Institute's founders. We People of Russell's Knob know who our forebears are. I grew up with these photos and the stories that accompany them. And I grew up knowing that, if the people of Russell's Knob were not more widely known and recognized in the mainstream, it could be attributed largely to racial prejudice. They were very interesting and accomplished people.

I have resisted digitizing. We've primarily given reprint

permissions to former students or faculty of The Institute, as if keeping them as family treasures. I enjoyed being covetous of them. Perhaps that's being "selfish", but in my mind I was proving to the ancestors that I was a staunch guardian of their legacy.

I have changed my mind on this point.

Love,
Ma

March 31, 2012

Dear Malcolm,

We've begun the initial phase of the digitization of the photographs. I now realize that digitizing does not diminish the photographs in any way. They are stunning in that format and Dr Campbell has done a superb job of contextualizing the collection, showing them at their best. She says that she's been ensnared by the photographs. And I think I've become ensnared as well. The preservation of the history of my ancestors and their beginnings in Russell's Knob has become, now that I've retired from the Institute, my life's work. *Life's work?* Somewhat self-important.

There are very few unidentified people in the collection. Brynne expressed surprise. Perhaps I've taken for granted that most all these people are known to me. She thinks it's a stunning achievement that my predecessor preserved and catalogued so much work identifying the people in our collection. Well, she was a brilliant and energetic woman and she built upon the work of others. I know I won't achieve as much as my mother, Dr. Barbara Elaine Madison, the mistress of archiving and preserving, who continued the work of her mother, Lillian Murtaugh Madison. However, I strive to be a faithful soldier in the Madison army of documenting and preserving.

Grandmother Lillian was influenced by the same feisty

determination to prove wrong all those who claimed that African-descended people had no history or accomplishments, had no preservable history, as Arturo Alphonso Schomburg, the renowned historian of African American culture was. They were acquainted. This is documented through the scholarly correspondence between them. Three letters in our collection are signed by him. Dr. Campbell and I must discuss where they should be displayed. I'm sure Mr. Schomburg is in heaven as pleased as punch that we honor him and that, through him and the library named for him, we have come to know so much about ourselves. I want Dr. Lillian Murtaugh Madison to feel similarly.

My grandmother always used the three names after her marriage. I'd like to make her more well known in her field. I'd also like to honor her mother, Pearl Miller Murtaugh, as well as Pearl's mother-in-law, my Gree-Gree, Lucille Murtaugh. What women they were! All of them. But for me Lucille Murtaugh is the linchpin, the most pivotal ancestor. She links our furthest past to this modern day.

I was raised to think that we family members had the responsibility to train ourselves to be bold and independent in every generation by building on the stubborn survivalist instincts of our forebears. This survivalism had always also meant the survival of the human mind and, for want of a better word, soul.

Our strange, outlier village always had a library, founded with Jacques Beaulieu's purloined library of books. Gree-Gree set down the traditional story that Beaulieu stole his slaveowner father's large library of books in French and English when he made his escape. He sold most all the

French volumes and installed the others in an outbuilding made of cedar wood in Russell's Knob. These earliest books in our collection are still beautiful and awe-inspiring.

The volumes are currently undergoing conservation. I hope their aroma does not change with conservation. I want the volumes still to smell of cedar, but I know they won't. We'll have to put them behind plexiglass in the museum. We can't have everybody breathing on them.

I'll have to remember the aroma. I admit that when the term "impermanence" is thrown about to crank up urgency for digitalization, I mention these volumes that, though paper, are extant. Cn thecedar smell be preserved on the cloud?

Those Beaulieu books form a nucleus of volumes collected and preserved by Lucille Murtaugh that includes texts used by his granddaughter in her little red schoolhouse. She bequeathed them to her amanuensis, Lucille and those collections became the first teaching materials used by the Williams-Murtaugh Institute for Colored Women's Education. These books are as much a part of me as the skin on my bones. This is our genealogy.

Well, I was left by myself with the duty to rescue, organize, and archive the books, documents, artifacts, and furnishings of the Institute. There's a lot of work to do, and there is just me. Not true. There is Dr. Campbell now, and there are others. Since you left - I say this as if you had a choice in it. I'm sorry- I'm alone. I'm bereft. Often, I am irritable and frightened and some days I don't feel like carrying on.

"It's a boil done come to a head." This is a quote I read somewhere. Or did it just spring into my head spontaneously because it is the kind of thing that ghostly presences do to reach us? I believe that. I think Mr. Lenny actually said this when we sat with the bourbon. He was right to chastise me. I didn't fix things that should have been fixed. Things came to a head when the river came over its banks.

Your Ma

April 1, 2012

"So, Posterity, if you are sufficiently, generationally
subsequent to me, then you will know who we
have become. If all proceeds as this humble
historian hopes, these journals, diaries, archives and
collections will endure and be an historical record
of us and will be consequential to our descendants
in the next century past the next. The twenty-first
century. Oh, Posterity, this is as far as I can imagine
you. Are you there?"

—Lucille Murtaugh, 1886

Dear M.,

Sometimes I write "Yes" in the upper left corner of the
pages of my journal. I feel directed as if I am answering
Lucille's questions. Yes, Gree-Gree, I am here. Your voice is
as clear as a bell reaching me through the generations, as if
tolled in your lifetime, but tolling still so many decades later.
I am proud to say I hear your bell. I am inhabited by you,
Lucille Murtaugh, and I am comfortable in your company.

Beloved Malcolm, are you my Posterity? If you are
deceased, are you still my generations or should I look
elsewhere? Your death was, in fact, the death of so many of
my goals. I mourn these, too. Motherhood, maternal energy
is our great elastic. The compelling movement back and

forward between our ancestors and our descendants is what makes us. We are someone's child and, depending on what life deals, could be someone's mother nurturer.

Often still, I think of something to make you aware of and get sad at my lost opportunity. I get a nearly unbearable pang of loss. It is brief thankfully. I feel disappointed with myself. See, that's the self-pitying part of it, the feeling that I am more bereft than any other person. Because, dear M., no one has ever loved a person more than I loved you. It is not possible. Saying that gives me comfort. Grieving deeply, tragically assures me that my love was appropriately deep as well. My great pain convinces me that I did love you enough, and this thought gives me a measure of comfort. So sometimes my gloomy feelings are uplifting to my spirits.

As time passes, I manage to move through the phases of these feelings more quickly and come to my even keel, my ordinary optimism. I'm confident that I can carry on until the time for my demise. I have an antidote for depression: My work. I must finish my work of preserving and documenting. I can't die tomorrow with the work undone.

Your Ma

April 4, 2012

Dear M.,

We've recovered other remains. We received word late yesterday that a casket had been identified as belonging to our cemetery and could be retrieved. I was startled by my own reaction to the recovery. It may be the one belonging to Lucille Murtaugh. I wept furiously. I hadn't allowed myself to register the awful feeling that her remaining remains had floated downstream and possibly out to sea even. Her headstone had been lifted and left feet from her grave. The cemetery was a shambles and several caskets were dislodged and misplaced. We hadn't yet identified which ones. This one was deposited by receding water in a back yard in a town downstream. We're only now beginning to put things right. Yesterday, between sobs I laughed at the Smoot-like drama of those caskets being churned up out of the earth and sent on a river voyage. Who knows where they might have ended up.

Dr. Campbell is applying for grants to study the dislodged remains. We want to hire a forensic archeology firm. Beloved Gree Gree floated off on an adventure, her casket going toward the Atlantic Ocean, riding massive swells, fortunate not to have gone under, though that is where she was bound for going, don't you think? So many others stayed in their plots even under duress of the wind and the water. Bu those waves dug up the sodden earth around certain graves like they were men with shovels. That old, exhausted dirt collapsed and shifted. Dynamic movement is what it was called by an engineer from the insurance company. The river lifted her out of her grave and Gree Gree headed for the City of Bones, in the middle of the Atlantic Ocean. Was she bound for visiting those millions on the ocean floor who never quite made it to the New World, those countless ones who perished at sea before reaching here? I'm paying the reward and sending a hearse to retrieve the casket.

Ma

April 8, 2012

Dear Malcolm,

It's Easter. If resurrection from the dead seems implausible, then spring flowers put a lie to that. Coming back from the dead seems absolutely possible in springtime. The backyard dogwood is beginning its stunning period, producing those achingly beautiful bracts. The wintertime branches are dull, a parody of dead, then boom the flowers pop back to life. Resurrection.

But I'll try not to push the metaphor too far. People who die don't return, resurrect. I don't care what the Bible says. Easter's, overwhelmingly hopeful concept that death is defeated by Jesus' action is a nice idea, but we bring Jesus back to life in our minds. All our beloveds are just as clearly divine and present as Jesus. Thinking of them makes it so. More in my case because I'm not a theist. I simply don't believe in Christianity or Islam or Judaism or any of the biggies anymore. I like Buddhism. What's not to like? I am disdainful of Zoroastrianism and Hinduism and Santeria. Ha, ha! What do I know of any of these? I suppose Animism would suit me.

I believe in you, Malcom Douglas.

Love,
Ma

April 9, 2012

M.,

The casket we believe to be Gree-Gree's has returned to the Old Smoot Cemetery. So much of spring and Easter is about dead back to life! And what a strange spring this has been. Destruction and rearrangement and reinternment and, all the while, the Dogwood is blooming, and jonquils are coming up. We have engaged a firm to examine the remains and advise us on the correct procedure for reinternment. At times I wish I was someone who could cling to religious belief. There would be rituals to cover this.

Love,
Ma

April 10, 2012

Dear M.,

In truth, I got a master's degree in social work rather than education because, back in the day, no self-respecting baby-boomer wanted to do the same things or be the same person as her mother. I went to work after college in the District of Columbia Department of Social Services as a social worker as my penance. It was a grim job, a grind that nevertheless taught me most of what I know now about education and about people who don't get any. I worked in that agency for ten years before I left to get the PhD.

While I was in graduate school, my mother convinced me to assume an associate directorship at The Institute and, though I insisted that I would not do it, she named me her successor as director. I didn't embrace the job at first, I simply did not refuse. She said she wanted to retire and resume her archival work. She said it was my responsibility to shepherd the school into the twenty-first century. I was sullen in my early years of the Directorship. I didn't smile much. I'm sorry now that I was angry and spiteful in those years. I eventually relaxed into the position.

Yes, we educated many young women and I am proud of the work we accomplished. Several of them are prominent in government, business, and education. I've spent most of my therapy sessions griping about my mother's manipulation of my career, but it was a good career. I did come to love my job.

M., I've been working on the forward to my history, as well as promotional material for the online project. I've worked myself into a lather on this: how to put into words what I was born knowing. Here's a bit of the fevered foreword:

The Williams-Murtaugh Institute is an educational institution, founded in 1905, which conferred baccalaureate degrees upon 6000 women before it closed its doors one hundred years later in 2005. The Institute's graduates are among the foremost African-identified women scholars, educators, and political figures in our nation. Its founders, having taught in schools for the formerly enslaved in the South and the North, founded their institution in Washington, D.C., and intended that it be a school for all those interested in improving their living circumstances through formal education and the acquisition of marketable skills in service and industry. It was created at the behest of the school's benefactor, Peter Williams.

M., I think this will do for the foreword. I will also write a chapter detailing include Peter Williams' backstory. It's a real adventure tale. I'm appalled at how little is known of our history, our Black peoples' history.

Love,
Ma

April 12, 2012

Dear M.,

I was seven years old on April 4, 1968, when Martin Luther King was assassinated. I hadn't remembered at first, but then the news reports brought it back. But I didn't want to reflect on it until today. The image that comes to me now when I reflect on the moment I had learned of his assassination is of me combing my hair. I was looking in the mirror above my mother's dresser. Her cosmetics, perfumes and jewelry were arrayed on the dresser. The television was on for the news, and I saw it in the mirror. I turned in horror. I remember thinking "How can people be so cruel?" Why do they hate us so?" It was us and them in those days. It's a date that will live in infamy for me, Malcolm. Perhaps now I will say that my choice of name for you was influenced by the names of our heroes: Marcus, Martin, and Malcolm.

Below is my chapter about Peter Williams. I am not surprised at ignorance, but I am struck by how little is taught in the schools of the heroism of the United States Colored Troops (USCT) in the American Civil War. I can give myself a migraine shaking my head in dismay and sucking my teeth in disgust at the narrowness of racism.

About Peter Williams, a.k.a. Petrus Wilhelm and the USCT:

Following the Civil War, Petrus Wilhelm returned home to Russell's Knob, New Jersey. He was a captain in the USCT, The United States Colored Troops. He achieved a captaincy, though so-called colored men were barred from the ranks above private, through subterfuge. He had a very White appearance, and his birth record stated his race as white.

Wilhelm's father listed his previous wife, a White woman, as his son's mother on the birth certificate. Though he clearly loved his second wife, Harriet Smoot Wilhelm, he was determined to give their child as much privilege connected to whiteness as he could manage. However, Petrus Wilhelm discovered this manipulation and he confronted his father about the lies. A letter written by Wilhelm to his father states his case for rejecting the privilege his father wanted to confer on him and is part of our document collection.

Fearing to be drafted into a company of Irish men like those who'd murdered his cousin — Jan Smoot had been a victim of the New York Draft Riots of 1863 — he enlisted in the USCT in Philadelphia. The recruiter who signed Petrus said it was a boon for the company if he would "pass" as a White man and rise in the ranks.

Wilhelm's expertise with firearms and his abilities to read and write were great assets. By all accounts he was an excellent captain and a compassionate man. His war experiences were harrowing, and he recorded them during the period of convalescence from his injuries. Wilhelm was wounded in action, and his left leg amputated below the knee by his friend, Dr. Ismail Murtaugh.

Shortly after he returned from visiting his father in Canada, after his discharge, he wrote to Dr. Murtaugh to urge him to relocate to Russell's Knob and open a medical practice. You will recall that Petrus' father prevented his pregnant mistress from being sold South and left his family in New Jersey when the two escaped to Canada. He remained there until his death.

Petrus Wilhelm and Ismail Murtaugh had forged a deep friendship through their war experiences. Also, Petrus Wilhelm had formed a deep emotional bond with Dr. Murtaugh's nurse, Naomi Coats. Wilhelm specifically asked that Dr. Murtaugh ask Miss Coats to relocate to Russell's Knob, too. In fact, he suggested that Dr. Murtaugh should "implore" Miss Coats to come. This letter is a part of the Williams-Murtaugh Institute's research archives.

The arrival of Dr. Ismail Murtaugh and Miss Naomi Coats at Russell's Knob in 1870 set in motion the circumstances that led to the creation of The Institute. Miss Coats, trained as a teacher at the Hampton Institute, had returned to her native Washington, D.C., during the Civil War. She worked as a laundress and nursing assistant in the contraband camps and medical tents of the Colored soldiers and returned to assist Dr. Murtaugh after the war in treating wounded men of the USCT. In this capacity,

Miss Naomi Coats became acquainted with Petrus Wilhelm. Since she was also trained as a teacher, she conducted classes for those wanting to learn to read. She read to wounded men and wrote letters as requested. Petrus Wilhelm wrote to his mother that he would never have recovered had it not been for Miss Naomi Coats and her calm, clear, lovely voice.

Captain Petrus Wilhelm married Naomi Coats. Their daughter, Mary Wilhelm is listed as born in 1875, but it is not clear if that year is correct. Around this time, Petrus became Peter and Wilhelm became Williams. Mary's name was changed and she is known in the Institute's archives as Mary Williams.

M., a note: Mary Williams died in 1896 in childbirth and is buried in a cemetery in Cincinnati, Ohio. We have discovered that she is the biological mother of Robert Murtaugh, Gree-Gree's son and is my biological great-great grandmother. I feel no less a part of Gree-Gree, Lucille Murtaugh. In fact, I'm tied the more closely to Peter Williams since he is Gree-Gree's brother as well as Robert's grandfather. My head is spinning! I have more relatives now that I know about.

Perhaps you are confused. I don't think that happens in your realm, but I will explain. You must remember that Petrus Wilhelm was a grown man when his sister, Lucille was born in 1875. His mother was quite young when he was born, and Lucille was her late-in-life baby. This will explain how Mary and Lucille became contemporaries.

My instincts were right about Lucille Murtaugh. I couldn't reconcile that she would give us so much detailed, intimate history of her entire family and not give us the most precious information about the patrimony of Robert Murtaugh. I feared the worst. Oh, the truth is distressing enough. Though they kept the secrets, as always, they set them down for the record. Robert Murtaugh's father is Reuben Closter.

Pearl Miller Murtaugh saved the excised journal entries and did not destroy them as her husband ordered her to do. I think we must genuflect and thank Pearl Miller Murtaugh for her preservation of the texts and for rescuing and saving the Russell's Knob Cemetery's records of burials.

We've referred to them in attempting to identify some remains. The first recorded burial is in 1798! All these documents were placed in a safe deposit box at The Industrial Bank of Washington in 1951 by Pearl Miller Murtaugh when her granddaughter, Barbara Elaine Madison was born.

These documents are the glue and yet I'd forgotten, overlooked them. My attention was called when the bank alerted us to the box when the branch was closing. I retrieved the documents. Dr. Campbell was thrilled at the records, and I was gratified to read the full story of Robert's birth and patrimony.

Lucille Murtaugh was a heroic woman in her age, in any age. And her devoted daughter-in-law, Pearl Miller Murtaugh defied her husband and preserved all Gree-Gree's papers and diaries rather than burn them as she'd promised her husband.

Your mother, a proud descendent

P.S. — This is the linchpin document. This posthumous

letter from Gree-Gree to Robert explains much. The loss, but not destruction, of the letter explains a lot, too. If Pearl Miller Murtaugh had not hidden these documents, had given in to her husband's wishes, we'd have missed vital information. Clearly, PMM was an archivist to her soul.

For Robert, upon my death:

Robert, legally your surname is Closter. Your father, Reuben Closter, married my cousin Mary, your mother, on her deathbed. She did not survive the day. You did. He left. Mary and I met Reuben Closter at Oberlin College in 1886. Reuben Closter and Mary began a courtship during our second year at Oberlin. Rules were strict, but Mary managed a rendezvous with Reuben, and the matron came in upon them in compromising circumstance. There was a furor and Reuben and Mary were asked to leave the school.

Mary had fallen completely under the spell of Reuben, and when they left Oberlin, she was confident that he intended to marry her, but he abandoned her in Cincinnati. She was, by this time, pregnant. The poor girl was left alone and destitute. I do not know how she survived all those months. I received two letters from her. She wrote brightly, cheerfully. I had no reason to be concerned.

Then I received a telegram from a boarding house proprietor who said that Mary was pregnant and alone and she was reluctant to take responsibility. I came immediately. Within three days of my arrival, Mary began a long, arduous labor. I made inquiries to find Reuben, and I engaged a doctor. Mary was in the midst of her labor when Reuben arrived at her bedside. He married her during a lull in her ordeal. I knew that Mary would die, and I was profoundly and irreparably affected by her loss.

We went to Oberlin because Father had attended there. Mary did not wish to study to be a teacher, but she was too shy to express her own opinion on any matter. I twisted her arms to go with me, knowing my parents were wavering at the thought of my going alone. The two of us together would be safe and our town needed teachers. Reuben was handsome as you are. He was tall, slim, black-haired, with hard black eyes that were then called beautiful, and he was of a lively temperament. He was in school to become a preacher, but after he left Oberlin, he continued schooling as a mortician.

With Love,
Your Devoted Mother

April 30, 2012

Dear M.,

Maroon New Jersey: The Complete History of Russell's Knob, the definitive text on the town and its people, is dedicated to Dr. Barbara Elaine Madison (1936 – 2011), director of The Williams-Murtaugh Institute from 1965 to 1990.

M., you know it all, all the facts and events, of course. But I can't help thinking that you want this conversation, this intercourse as much I do. Wishful thinking! In fact, I need it. I must have this exchange to keep going forward. Why shouldn't I keep you alive and nearby? Why can't I keep your face before me? And, as Barbara Elaine Madison often said: Life is lived in one direction only - forward. For a historian, that was a whacky statement. But mother believed that trying to live in the past was counter-productive even in pursuit of information about the past. Pursuing historical inquiry was, for her, building a highway to the future.

Your grandmother was a graduate student in history at Howard University when she learned she was pregnant. She married my father, Anthony Douglas, her professor of history who had completely swept her off her feet. She left her studies, settled down to be a housewife and waited for me to come. I did. She returned to studying and teaching soon after my birth and her husband left soon after that. Anthony Douglas became a "firstie," the first Black professor at a certain Midwestern college. He climbed to a tenured professorship and never looked back. My mother completed her masters, became the assistant director for student life at the Williams-Murtaugh Institute, obtained a doctorate in history from the University of Pennsylvania and succeeded Lillian Murtaugh Madison to the directorship of the Institute in 1965.

I think of myself as being very like her and I'm proud of that. She was my model in all things. She named me Amarantha because she had a lively imagination and, as she said, because she felt all the names my father suggested were too staid. What must his choices have been to be staider than Amarantha? His mother was born on St. Croix, so likely Odette or Odilie. But, of course, Amarantha has always sounded like just the name for the director of a school for young women founded at the dawn of the twentieth century.

Mother did like to tease me about my name. She reminded me often that the purple amaranth is a weedy, worrisome plant to most people. Though it is grown in other parts of the world as an edible plant, it's thought to be a nuisance in the U.S. It is included in Lucille Murtaugh's almanac of edible plants accompanied by a drawing. I am awed by the sheer volume of work that L. M., my beloved Gree-Gree, accomplished in her lifetime and the variety of her skill set. My goodness, I suppose Mother went all the way back to Gree-Gree's almanac, whether intentionally or subconsciously, to get that name. She gave me a unique name, heavily freighted with meaning and history, but easy enough to tote.

I had a close relationship with my mother. In fact, I had many relationships with my mother. I was her daughter, her employee, her colleague, her successor, her assistant, and her nurse. I only balked at being her replacement as director of The Institute. However, I found it was a wonderful job. I had a few crises. I handled them satisfactorily. Most of the directorship was rewarding once I'd settled in.

The challenge has been in hewing to our core, founding purpose in the so-called post-racial era. We are no longer needed in the traditional ways. The times have, thankfully, changed. Our enrollments are down. Our typical student has, since the late '60s, had more options for higher education. An institution that is completely dedicated to the education and enrichment of African American women is still needed, still vital. We've been slow to change.

Now we've embarked on an exciting new educational opportunity. We are becoming the Williams-Murtaugh Institute for the Continuing Education of All People. We will be a completely online university. We intend to have a wonderfully interactive curriculum emphasizing a concentration on the African presence in the Atlantic World. We will be open to all who are open to us.

We've given up the bricks and mortar buildings in Washington, D.C. Those lovely old buildings on Georgia Avenue, built in the early 1900's, are becoming an apartment complex. All the Institute's collections are being archived and digitized. We are creating a museum in the Nineva VanWaganen House once we've catalogued and done some restorations and renovations. We've received funds to continue restoration of this building, the oldest original structure in Russell's Knob. Photographs of the work on the Nineva VanWaganen House can be found at the Institute's website and on our Facebook page. Hah!

Can you believe it, M? I'm excited. The undertaking is ambitious, and it frightens me a bit. But now is the time. This transition to the online university will get us out from under the real estate. Having to have a certain critical mass of students to compete for teacher salaries with the so-called elite universities has been exhausting us financially and otherwise. Now that African American women scholars are being hired in these places, we've had more competition. The chief benefit we were able offer faculty was a strong academic community in a vibrant urban environment and our excellent students. What we are marketing to our next faculty and student community is the vibrancy of an online university with our unique, historical brand. Enrollment at Williams-Murtagh will give the student a measure of our legacy. I think our ancestors, the oldest of the old, will be happy with the plan.

The People of Russell's Knob and their descendants have never wanted to disappear, but just to live undisturbed by White hostilities. We have always had clever children and we've wanted them to learn and shine and thrive. To that end the people of Russell's Knob lived a Maroon existence until after the American Civil War. Then Lucille Murtaugh put them onto her shoulders and carried them into the twentieth century by collecting their everything and researching and cataloguing and archiving all their books, papers, Bibles, furniture, and ephemera. She set to educating as many promising, young, Colored women as she encountered.

I'm proud to be the descendent of this remarkable woman. She trod a path through hardship with intelligence and grace. Many other women did, too, though they did not have her wit and determination and her passion for history.

M., I think I have done much less for my people. I tell myself that there was so much more to do in her day, so much more urgency. They had to stop lynching. Women had to get the vote. There is urgency in the twenty-first century, too. Some of the same urgencies, truth be told. Still our dark people are being cut down in the streets. Our African-descended people have still not been able to shake off the disdain of the White world. The White world is surely shrinking, but the impact of colorism still pounds people down to dust.

And so, I judge myself, M., and rightly so. What have I done that has benefitted The People? I think I'm at the place many get to. I'm doing a lot of summing up and wondering if I've got the energy to redouble my efforts because I'm not sure I've done enough.

Please don't abandon me to self-pity, M. If your voice leaves me, I will go to the cliff and jump. Oh, yes, I know this is but an echo I hear so that I will not sink into a slurry of depression. I am always tempted to wear my sadness. If I scowl folks will know I loved you more than I love ice cream or delight or laughter or sunrise. I know you would say my career as an educator has been of great service to my people, specifically for The People I am most concerned about. Yes, you are right. My career as an educator has been a purposeful vocation, a meaningful one. Thank you for reminding me of this. Still, I yearn for you.

Ma

May 1, 2012

Dear Malcolm,

Dr. Campbell is working furiously on her book project of the town's photographs which includes portraits of nineteenth century residents. M., watching her curation process is fascinating. The photos are stunningly beautiful, rather the people are beautiful. Yet, it's true that the photos themselves are beautiful, artful. Dr. Murtaugh had a talent for photography. The most beautiful single photo in the collection is Dossie Smoot's wedding photo though it was taken by a photographer working professionally in Paterson. You remember it. I have a copy in a frame on my desk.

M., Dossie Smoot was, without a doubt, a beautiful woman. I am sure she was greatly admired for her looks back in her day. We have only two photographs of Dossie in our collections. She had the most perfect wasp waist. There is a corset from the nineteenth century that is said to have belonged to her. However, it's not likely she was wearing the thing in her wedding photo. We have a creepy funeral photo of her at her final rest. I hope there will be at least one more to be found among the many yet undeveloped gelatin plates belonging to Dr. Murtaugh. We have begun to process those remaining ones that haven't fallen victim to the passage of time. The majority were well preserved.

It is her face in the wedding photograph that is so

compelling to me. She manages to appear naive, hopeful, quiet, eager, wise, and sexy all at once. Quite a feat! She came to be thought of as a strange and unapologetically powerful woman in Russell's Knob.

Ma

May 16, 2012

Dear M.,

I'm digging into some of the letters in our collection. Specifically, Dr. Campbell and I are looking at Petrus Wilhelm/Peter Williams' Civil War period correspondence. I am building a portrait of our founder. He was a complicated man, but he adored his sister. He provided for her vocation and secured a comfortable future for her. Though she is often very frank about his character, she clearly loved him as well.

We've arranged to donate the oil portrait of Petrus Wilhelm that hung in The Institute's main hall since the founding to The Newark Museum. It is a painting by Robert Scott Duncanson and is a valuable work. It is documented that Duncanson had a connection to Wilhelm/Williams and his family. Duncanson's work is receiving renewed interest lately and he is now considered a founding member of The Hudson River School of landscape painters. This portrait was commissioned for the Institute and was a gift from the artist. It will make an excellent accompaniment to the other Duncanson painting in Newark museum's collection, *Mountain Landscape with Cows and Sheep.* More about that Duncanson connection later.

M., I wish I had a nickel for each time I had to give the Petrus Wilhelm/Peter Williams lecture. Each crop of newbies had to be told that the portrait of the White-looking man was, in fact, Lucille Murtaugh's brother and that he'd lived his entire life as a mixed-race man and that he'd bequeathed his estate to the education of African-descended women. The first of many lectures on not judging books by their covers. And I generally add, Robert Scott Duncanson, the artist, was a mixed-race man who was a successful painter in his day. Williams was a man of his times. And men like him - men who are mixed race - were not as rare as some might suggest. There are a sizeable number of people who now live as Whites who have African blood.

Pondering their colors, studying the photographs, M., one understands that families in Russell's Knob are not easily grouped or understood by their colors. There's variety in most of the families. It becomes *not* how they think of themselves, The People.

Ma

May 17, 2012

Dear M.,

I thought I would never admit that I have regrets. I try not to "go there," as you would say. But I do regret not having shared some of this family history with you. You wondered why I made such a big thing of writing letters. It's because we have letters from our ancestors and can use them to substantiate the picture of the town. The correspondence is the glue that holds a lot of our history together, the personal and the families'. If I had known that time would run out on us, I would have filled you to the brim with these letters, I think.

Here is a letter from Wilhelm to his sister, Lucille that gives you a measure of him.

February 20, 1887

Dear Luce, Dear Girl,

Why do you want me to recount my war days?
What are you doing, girl? What do you intend,
Lucille? Your father says that you are writing a great
book about him and me and our exploits in the war.
He says that you are endeavoring to write a thorough,
historical account of our town and that the "great war
against slavery" accounts are just the beginning.

Well, you are the right one to do the ferreting out of the stories. You are a nosey-posey. You are a hardheaded, smarty-pants girl who thinks she can do everything imaginable as a man can. Do you still squat to pee? I wonder if you know that women in other towns are not so bossy as the ones here in Russell's Knob? Do you intend to marry? Do you think a man wants to have a wife who is brainier than he is? Do you think you should use up your youthful and most beautiful years on this pursuit? Perhaps you ought to postpone writing these stories until your grandchildren begin asking for tales on chilly evenings. Do not lock yourself away reading old letters and writing books. Go out to the beer garden and the dances and all the socials and let one of the smart, successful men offer you a marriage and a home.

I think your father feels the same as I do but is too indulgent of you to be frank. Frankly, Luce, you should put off this history undertaking until after you've married and started up a baby or two. Writing histories is for old women and old men. Remembering stuff and dragging up the past is something you can do when the bloom is off.

Frankly, Luce, you have the cudgel. I love our mother and I love your father as though he were my own, too, and as a brother. I love you and so you may ask anything of me. I will be slow and sullen though. You will have to wheedle. You are also accomplished at wheedling. That is why I say

you ought to marry: you have all the requisites; you
have a pretty face; you have a lovely body and you
are an expert at wheedling.

Your devoted,
PW

May 18, 2012

Dear M.,

Franky, frankly, frankly, he writes. I am always charmed by Wilhelm's letter-writing style, but what folderol.

I'm touched by Lucille Murtaugh's journals and diaries, M. I've yet to admit this openly, but I consider that it is to me directly that she's speaking. I am her posterity. I am her "friend in the future." I get chills thinking of it, reading her words, in her sweet, neat hand. I am so proud that we've reached the 21st century. And I can be proud that her papers, her accounts and her records and books and collections and things, have come down through the generations.

So, when I read Petrus Wilhelm's question about "Why do you want this?" I want to slap him behind the head and say, "Why do you think, numb nuts?" But, because he gave all his support and lots of wealth to Lucille, his brilliant, eccentric, obsessive, driven half-sister who collected and archived our available past and enshrined it at The Institute, preserving it for her "posterity," I am tolerant of him. And I thank him for the money.

Lucille Murtaugh was hard-headed and courageous, and she was also a single mother. Her posterity was assured only narrowly. Though Robert Murtaugh is said to have been her adopted child. I've guessed that he was, in fact, the out-of-wedlock child of Lucille.

There is absolutely no evidence of the identity of the father of Robert Murtaugh. And, amidst all this scrupulous archiving, there is no birth certificate for Robert Murtaugh. It is unbelievable that, in all the papers and letters and accounts by a person driven to record and document, there is no mention of the identity of her son's father. Even in maintaining the fiction of a cousin being Robert's true mother, Lucille does not ever even hint at his paternity. Lucille is so eloquent and is not shy about speaking of loves and trysts and humiliating behaviors. Why doesn't she write something about her lover, about this child's father? Could the official story of Robert Murtaugh's birth be true?

According to the stories as generally told, nobody really believed that he was anyone but Lucille's child. Lucille was said to have been visiting her father's relatives in Cincinnati and, out of the goodness of her nature, returned with an unfortunate orphan to raise as her own. However, it is plausible in that she would have felt the necessity of providing for a family member, a vulnerable child.

I shudder to think that the reason for her omission of this information is that it is connected to violence and humiliation. I'm going to have to consider that possibility whether I want to or not.

M., one thing that intrigues me as I ruminate on these personal twists and turns of our ancestors is this: You must now know. You know all these bits of our fabric. You know all the answers I long for. I wonder why I'm doing so much earthly longing. I'll get the fulsome story when I reach there, right? Or is there still mystery? If it is all revealed at that sudden, inevitable moment of crossing over, then why am

I pursuing this amalgamation of our earth-bound history?
Can't wait to die or morbidly afraid to? I must be the one to
put it all together for the generations after us.

Self-importance. Family obsession.

More from Gree-Gree, M.:

February 28, 1887

Dear Posterity,

He was right. I have had to beg and wheedle
and plead to get all his stories. I think I did learn
all I wanted to know of his war and post-war
experiences from the writings - mostly letters,
a great many love letters between him and Aunt
Naomi. He also wrote long accounts of battle
engagements and about getting wounded and being
saved by Father.

The love letters told me a good deal about the
man, too. I felt differently about him, after reading
them. He had loved Naomi. I did not doubt it after
reading the letters he wrote to her. But he was not
kind to her. And he is one of those people who can
separate the two. I suspect that, in marriage, very
often kindness and love come loose from each other
and bear no real relation over time. Of course, he
began very soon after his marriage to subjugate and
deceive Naomi. And though our town has many
powerful, independent women, a man is given
unquestioned authority over his wife and children

here. Oh, how lucky is she who has an intelligent, courageous, compassionate, and fair father!

Lucille Murtaugh

May 25, 2012

Dear M.,

I suppose I'm trapped in it. I'm jealous of you ancestors, but I've got work to do. I've got a deadline for pulling together this chapter: The Civil War Accounts of Ismail Murtaugh and Petrus Wilhelm. Their story is exciting and their unique perspectives on the war are compelling. I just need to come up with a better title.

 From my text:

By the time Company C the 8th Regiment United States Colored Troops met their final engagement in Virginia, all of the soldiers in Captain Wilhelm's company knew he was no true White man no matter what he looked like or the Army said. They knew he was a Black African in his soul. Company C became the regiment's gutty core, a fierce, implacable force under the command of Captain Petrus Wilhelm. He emerged as a true leader. He prepared his company well. He improved on some combat techniques and drilled soldiers relentlessly in handling their arms. The men under his command understood that he was entirely comfortable with them and considered them to be like himself and that their lives were valuable, that they were not army fodder, that they had a claim to stake and a name to make.

In fact, it seemed that Captain Wilhelm preferred his men's company to that of other White officers. The men of Company C chided him for sitting and eating with them at night instead of with the officers. They asked his friend, Dr. Murtaugh to suggest that Wilhelm ought to sit with the other Whites so they wouldn't discover his secret. His company wanted to keep him and his secret.

The men in his company were also impressed with his survival skills. He had grown up a coddled boy by the standard of circumstance of most of his company. They were, by and large, men who had been in bondage. He'd been taught a lot and toughened up by his uncle. He had hunted game and fished and climbed rocky terrain and looted canal barges, dressed game, and handled horses and mules. He had owned and cared for guns and knives. The men of Company C were surprised to see how many knives he carried on his person. Wilhelm had been accustomed, since childhood, to hiding weapons in his clothes.

M., I am stumped. The narrative of Wilhelm and Murtaugh's adventures does not flow. I have decided to set down events simply, bluntly, raggedly and then organize and fill in the gaps.

Petrus Wilhelm enlisted in the USCT in Philadelphia as did his friend, whom he did not know at the time, Ismail Murtaugh.

Of Dr. Murtaugh and Wilhelm's leg:

Their regiment fought in the Peninsula Campaign in Virginia. Company C became trapped behind Confederate lines. Wilhelm was shot in the lower portion of his leg as he carried a wounded man to a defensive position. Dr. Murtaugh treated the Captain's wound and gave him whatever battlefield medical care he could.

The two were cut off from the other members of their company when their position was run over by Confederates, and the men had had to retreat under fire. They killed some of the Confederates including a captain. Wilhelm and Murtaugh took shelter in a cave until. Under cover of darkness, Dr. Murtaugh changed Wilhelm from his Union blues into the dead Confederate captain's uniform, and carefully bound up their Union uniforms. The doctor adopted the clothes and demeanor of a personal slave, putting Captain Wilhelm aboard a Confederate medical wagon. Running beside the wagon, never faltering, Dr. Murtaugh was there with him for the entire thirty-mile journey so that Wilhelm would not betray himself by calling out in delirium.

Murtaugh amputated the captain's leg himself when they reached the field hospital because he knew they dared not wait any longer. He doused Wilhelm with laudanum and saved his life outside of Richmond.

After the capture of Richmond on April 2, 1865, Wilhelm and Murtaugh rejoined their regiment and learned of the losses in their heroic company. When Captain Wilhelm was scheduled to be transferred to a military hospital for White officers, he protested and insisted that he ought to be sent to the Freedman's Hospital in Washington, D.C., where the wounded men of his company were taken. He did, in effect, reveal his racial identity. He was sent to the Freedman's Hospital for treatment, but he kept his racial status in the regimental records. After the war, Dr. Murtaugh was allowed to practice on the staff of this hospital though his credentials had not been recognized before the war.

Neither Captain Wilhelm nor Dr. Murtaugh received the military honors they might otherwise have received, i.e. if they were White men, but both received their military pensions. Captain Wilhelm had his pension signed over to the wife of a man of his company, Pompey Norfolk, who died at The Peninsula after saving several others and whose papers were lost in an administrative snarl that Wilhelm blamed on himself.

Often it is said that when a man returns from war, he is a different man altogether. Not so for Petrus Wilhelm. He returned home not as a different man, but more a concreted version of himself. He was tougher, more hedonistic, more ruthless, and aggressive in his business concerns and, out of the shade of his more handsome, dead cousin, he was thought to be more attractive.

I adore Gree-Gree's description of the Wilhelms:

How on earth can a brown sparrow hiding among the leaves ever hope to hold onto a barrel-chested robin strutting about for worms? Ah! The more he is punished by his sparrow, the more profligate he becomes. He thinks he is owed some fun after all. The war, the leg. His misbehavior is allowed. He disgusts me at times, and I've said so. He replies good-naturedly always. "You're a girl, Luce. You don't know anything about men." He is a fool and an idiot! Naomi is an idiot for allowing him to behave with her as he does.

So not a love match. Gree-Gree's parents, however, were certainly a love match, a love-at-first-sight kind of match. When Harriet Smoot Wilhelm and her brother came to Washington to see Petrus at the Freedman's Hospital, Dr. Murtaugh is said to have been struck completely dumb at the first sight of Harriet with her son. Though he knew Wilhelm's family history, he was surprised to see that The Smoots were Brown. Harriet, still young, was known to have been beautiful. Clearly, feelings of passion were mutual between them. Was it simply gratitude that Ismail Murtaugh had saved her son's life? No. By all accounts, Harriet Murtaugh was deeply in love with her husband and he with her. Gree-Gree's writing is filled with references to their physical affection and, with a whiff of envy, her own disappointments with intimacy.

So, M., Wilhelm then was the great architect of Russell's

Knob's post-war identity. He coerced his friend to come to practice medicine in the town. On the marriage pf Dr. Ismail Murtaugh and Harriet Smoot Wilhelm, he deeded the Wilhelm house to his mother and Dr Murtaugh and built a house for himself and his wife on a ridge nearby on land adjoining the brewery property. It is important to note that he did that, deeded the land. It has been vital that our ancestors have been meticulous, scrupulously careful to document their legal rights. This holds even in the case of documents which contain untruths, i.e. Petrus Wilhelm's birth certificate and Dossie Smoot's marriage license, not to mention the great obfuscations in cemetery records.

A town center began to emerge as Wilhelm built a two-room schoolhouse and Dossie Smoot leased a structure nearby, making renovations and using it for a general store. Wilhelm constructed an office and a surgery for Dr. Murtaugh's medical practice. Naomi then began to teach an elementary course of study for the town's children and an additional teacher was hired. Three years after her daughter Mary was born, Naomi retired from teaching and two Oberlin graduates were hired. Mensah Paul let rooms for the teachers opening the first boarding house in Russell's Knob in 1880.

So, I think the next twenty years were a peaceful, productive period for the People of Russell's Knob. They continued to maintain their hyper-vigilance though there was more commerce with the town of Paterson. Lucille's and Mary's childhood would have been quite privileged. They grew up well-cared for and well educated. Sarah Jane Smoot, too. They were nurtured by their outsider, autonomous town.

M., read this: "The Presentiment of Lucille Murtaugh." This journal entry is a linchpin. Gree-Gree sets out the template for all of this, this historiography. I ought to have shared this with you earlier.

January 4, 1900

Dear Posterity,

We have a new century! We have been embarrassingly festive in our town since the first day of this new century. Though we use any excuse to frolic, you cannot blame us kicking up our heels for the twentieth century begun. We townspeople celebrated at the beer garden. Many hearts and hands and other such entwined in its bushes. Alas, not me.

Ah, the heart cannot help but be hopeful as time marches into a new era. Will there be a new era of peaceful coexistence for our people? I worry. Often now I muse on you, Posterity. Following the loss of the old ones of Russell's Knob, I feel like a rudderless skiff. Which way forward? Forward at all costs because you are there.

Are you? If this writing has reached you, my Posterity, you are probably chuckling at my worries and speculations. You can, no doubt, say, "Great-grandmother, of course, I am here." I know you are there, Posterity, even if you are completely unaware of me yet. Our people are survivors. You would have managed, despite any obstacles including the loss of my diaries, to be alive and thriving. I know you.

"Obstacles, Great-Grandmother? Our people are here and fully free and successful. There are no differences in our country's citizenry. Each one has a vote and a chance."

Will we women have, by your era, organized ourselves into a formidable block of voters? It is inevitable that we will have the right to vote someday. Will we elect some others than the screaming warmongers that we now have? Things cannot continue as they are with drunken louts able to choose our officeholders, while sober, upstanding women cannot. Our colored men have wrung out some slice of their rights as citizens. Why shouldn't we women? The men fear we will be able to sweep our candidaes into office on a wave of contagious hysteria. I've heard this said. How foolish! Women are not aligned in one single block and would hardly all vote as one. Likely many will fall under the influence of a man and vote accordingly. I do know my sex when they are uneducated, are unaware. Surely there will be a woman who is president of our country by your time. I know you are a wise, well-educated, benevolent person, Posterity. You are my descendant, and I am convinced that those important and essential attributes that determine us were bequeathed to you by our ancestors as they were to me. The unfortunate ones as well. Are you as prone to criticize others as I am? If you

are Smoot-Murtaugh descended, you do not suffer
fools gladly, and you are filled with the stuffing
to tell anyone this is so. Perhaps I should pray
that you are not too single-mindedly, obstinately
determined to be proud that you run afoul of
some hostile opponent and do not survive. As I've
watched my beloved ones go, I no longer fear for
my survival, but for yours. My ancestors and yours
have survived more challenges than either of us is
likely to encounter, and I feel confident I can meet
what comes because I am cut from their cloth.
We are sturdy. I hope you are as well, though it is
pointless for me to worry about you, you who has
not yet been, who may not be. You are a person
who prizes the life of the mind and who believes
that our people must ever be attentive to improving
themselves so that they cannot be excluded from the
privileges of citizenship. I know this. This belief is
your natural legacy. This belief is fed to you with
your mush. We have been people who demanded
respect. Are we still?

Is it necessary still to be? Are you also a
recalcitrant, a person who will not be quiet until
all are equally free? To the degree that it is still
necessary to be, I hope that you are recalcitrant.
Commitment to personal enrichment is what I
wish for my generations. I hope that you are a
sage and that you have been a staunch defender of
our family's legacy. I wish this for you more than
beauty or wealth. I want you to be brave enough

to carry your children out of bondage, keep them
alive and bring them to a mountain Elysium as my
ancestor, Lucy Smoot did. I hope you are patient
and persistent and have read so far as this. I realize
that I am asking you to depart from your life and its
progress to consider my life. What hubris! Why stop
your life because of a persistence in looking back
over the lives of your forebears? But if you read this
document, you may gain insights that you might not
otherwise have and can save some of your valuable
lifetime in discovering what is already known. You
have been born within me. You have been with me
and my thoughts for a long while. Yes, I believe
this is so. I have already brought you to life in
my mind. Can you keep open one corner of your
consciousness for speculating on me and the other
ancestors as I have speculated on you? It has just
this day become 1900. May I muse on our future,
upon your life in your time? The net result of this
musing will, undoubtedly, be a boon rather than
otherwise. I enjoy wondering if we may approach
each other at some place outside of the ordinary
time, each yearning for the other, each straining
toward the other. Apologies in advance for having
stolen these precious moments. I think of life as a
ball, round, filled with air. Rolling along the ground
it is not moving in an orderly way, a line forward.
It is liable to go in an infinite progression of back
to forward and side to side and sometimes gently
undulating downhill and sometimes stalled, washed

into a gully, but a stopping point is inevitable because progress is always arrested by fate. Round and round and forward and back we go until we meet that wall beyond which our body will not go, and our body is sloughed off to free up our soul that goes off like a butterfly to light upon another corporeal being.

I have wondered if one's people or family group or clan get a certain number of souls allotted and must circulate them to descendants as they become available. Happily, this pool is ever widening. Does a piece of the familial soul always remain? I've come to this belief though I have none but anecdotal proof that it is so. Have you received some part of my soul, loved one? Aha! In that case, I am on my notice. I must keep this soul clean, unburdened by ignorance and ignominious behavior. I will be good for your sake then.

I am writing to you, Posterity, because you are my governor now. I am bereft of my parents and others. I must be guided now by the impulse to make this world a better place for Robert and his descendants down to you. I want to present myself to you. As I sit here, I imagine myself with you as you read of me. If I am embodied here in this text, caught like a bug in an amber drop, then you will recreate me mentally. I would like that.

Recording our village's history gives my life an important purpose. I hope that no fire or flood or plague of locusts consumes my journals and my

collections. I am doing my best to preserve them for
the twenty-first century. I have put the completed
volumes of my journal into cedar chests. Are there
too many of them? I have several large containers
that were made to preserve books, papers, and
vulnerable ephemera.

Of course, if you are reading this, you know
about the journals in the cedar chests and the herbs.
I pray that you will receive them directly into
your hands from a relative who is following my
request that my journals be given to a person in
each generation of the Smoot-Wilhelm-Murtaugh
descended who will preserve them. It is a conceit!
It is one woman's obsession, and it is the all-
consuming passion of her life now that her parents
are deceased. Robert, my beloved son, is my only
other passion. Robert is my great joy.

My half-brother, Petrus Wilhelm is White
in appearance. If distinctions such as this no
longer matter in your time, then I am pleased. Pet
resembles his German father and, in our America,
this gives him a considerable advantage. Many
like him have passed seamlessly into White towns,
mingled in, and taken advantage with little regret.
However, Petrus wears this appearance like a cloak,
a mask. He has always been my mother's son inside
himself, a true Smoot.

What is a Smoot, never mind a true one? We are
the descended of Lucy Smoot, also known as Lucy,
the Angolan and her husband, Russell Sitton, the

founder of Russell's Knob. Have our people been able to slough off the legacy of their enslavement in this land? I can imagine it. I like to imagine it. It is because I choose to imagine this equilibrium in your century that I am recording my time. To honor the struggles of our ancestors to gain citizenship rights and to thrive, I am recording and preserving the history of the people of Russell's Knob, who thrived in defiance of slavery and Black codes.

I hope I will live to see the vote for women. I hope you will be looking back and marveling that it had taken so long for the power brokers to yield to our gentle though sharp intellects. What woman is not, at the very least, the equal of a man? Most of us are far cleverer.

In our town, there are many stories of epic journeys. Funny that is. We have been insular, very, very insular until the beginning of this century. I am in the vanguard of those who went away to school, to work and to wander. Residents are, for the first time, moving away to larger towns with more to offer their children. We can now live comfortably and openly in most towns.

A caveat: In Washington, D.C., on a visit, we enjoyed a lively, stimulating life in Colored society. There were, however, many places from which we Colored were barred. In our Nation's Capital! Racially motivated conflicts are found in all the northern towns. And in the southern cities, towns, hamlets, backwaters, bayous, and byways, there is the abominable practice of lynching.

I worry about Robert constantly. The more our children raise their heads and their voices and ask to be admitted to the mainstream, the more they are rebuked. Ah, we must cultivate a subservient manner or be daily challenged, upbraided, humiliated, threatened. How do we continue to tell our children to withstand the storm and persevere if there is no reward? Though he is only four years old, I know Robert will be a brilliant student. He is my son. Yet, he is Colored, and this is all they will think about. I is all they will wish to know about him.

I am indignant that we are always struggling to gain a place at the White peoples' table in this country. But where else can we be? We are the people of this place. Our blood has soaked into this ground. Some of the we of us have always been here.

Since when is when. Huh!

Note: this is a native phrase in our town: "Since when is when. Huh!" I have written in this "huh!" It is not a word said, but a sound appended to the phrase. You may imagine what it means.

I spent the entire year of 1898 affixing names to the photographs and photographic plates of Dr. Ismail Murtaugh, my beloved father. Photographs without names are historically useless. Even if, as some believe, a photograph captures the subject's soul, whose soul was it? I consulted Father's

records, searched newspapers, and made inquiries.
For each, there is identification. A full year's work.
Have they remained intact? Oh, how will I know?
I will have to visit you. Surely you see why. I will
haunt you gently though, I promise.

Don't close the book here, Posterity. I am
teasing you. I am just praying that nothing destroys
Father's photographs and that I have done all I
can to preserve them. If I can discern this without
disturbing your peace, I will. Of course, I allow
for the possibility that, when I reach the other
side of the death curtain, I will see that previously
unimagined properties obtain. I will know more
of life and death. Consequently, I prefer to dream
optimistically, to imagine hopefully. You are there
or will be. I am positing that I will be available to
you. I hope you are with me here, with these pages.

Perhaps you will be still living on our beautiful
mountain. Your head bowed to the page; I see you.
You are there, here, or will be. I will attempt to
reach you through whispers and apparitions and
tapping. Be aware, but please don't be frightened
or offended. My intention will be your survival. I
will revisit this realm if I'm able. I hope we will
recognize each other. I firmly believe, though it
makes my head spin to think about it, you are there,
here, or will be, as am I.

Fact: I have had no credible visitations from
my ancestors. Occasionally a flock of birds lifting
to the air will remind me of some aphorism or

witticism uttered by an ancient that has passed
to me. I do, of course, often imagine that I hear
Mother's or Father's voices. Mary cries out
occasionally. Old Noelle Beaulieu upbraids me in a
disgusting combination of pidgin French and Jersey
Dutch that I simply do not understand and cannot
attribute to anyone else. All of this remains in my
brain though. I have not ever seen a corporal figure
returned. I intend to participate in a seance just to
satisfy myself that there is nothing to be gained.
My goodness I've spun a fantastical yarn. Perhaps I
ought to have a bit more sherry and retire. Perhaps I
should have had less sherry.

Your Friend in the Future,
Lucille Murtaugh

May 26, 2012

Dear M.,

"I know you are a wise, well-educated, benevolent
person, Posterity. You are my descendant, and I
am convinced that those important and essential
attributes that determine us were bequeathed to you
by our ancestors as they were to me."

—Lucille Murtaugh

I have written this on a card I keep on my desk. I truly
believe I am the one she intended to reach with her words
and her things. Heartbreakingly, Lucille Murtaugh died
suddenly in 1933. Rilla, her companion dog, never again ate
a meal. She could not be urged, begged, or forced to eat. Her
grief was so profound that she died within a week of Mother
Lucille's death.

Our dogs, too, have an extant genealogy, for the most
part. Our Beverly has an ancestor of legendary beauty. He
continues to this day as the advertising icon of the Franklin
Sporting Goods Company's True Blue high velocity shotgun
shells. He was known as Blue Black and his image has been
used for decades as the finest example, the most beautiful
black lab who has ever lived, to hawk this product. Those
amber eyes are so compelling that I would buy some shells
though I have no shotgun and absolutely no interest in killing

game. Despite her breed's name, neither does Beverly have a desire to retrieve game. But Blue Black has long been a symbol of hunting prowess, shooting skills. Ah! That blue black head of Blue Black is still on tin signs everywhere in the upstate hunt country.

The story of how we became connected to that illustrious ancestor is a delight. A velvet black puppy was one of eight in the litter that yielded Blue Black. Petrus Wilhelm was by this point known as Peter Williams. And Peter Williams' friend, Erasmus Franklin, was a renowned hunter of upland game. On a visit to Russell's Knob, he brought a puppy to his friend, extolling its value as a retriever of game. Williams accepted the dog because he was eager to cultivate a social connection to Franklin. He gave the dog to Lucille, and the animal was named, Sassafras. This began a lifelong association between Lucille and canine companions. After Sassafras came two more, a daughter called Sassy and a granddaughter called Frassy. These were followed by Frassy's son, a dog called Buster, and he was followed by two more beloved direct descendants, one called Perry and Lucille's last companion, the much beloved, Rilla. We can trace Bev's descent directly from these ancestors who were related to the celebrity advertising icon.

Queenie, a direct descendent of Rilla was presented to Dr. Barbara Elaine Madison when she returned to Russell's Knob in 1958 as a symbol of the sacred bond between the people of Russell's Knob and their dogs and because a pregnant woman living alone in a big and remote house needed a companion dog. When she came back to Russell's Knob to research her history of The People and settle at the

Smoot-Wilhelm homestead, Dr. Madison was presented with Queenie, Beverly's four times great-grandmother. Dr. Madison and Queenie were inseparable. Queenie had four litters with six puppies in each.

In her third litter, Basil was born, and he alone remained with his mother in the home with Dr. Madison and became my very best friend. Basil was a "rounder" and had many puppies around the area. The loss of Basil was my first grief, first heartbreak.

When he was struck and killed by an automobile, a daughter of his was identified by her coal-black velvet coat, her amber eyes, her leathery nose and gentle, intelligent nature and she was adopted and came to live with us. She was Ruby. I would have named the new dog something else, but she'd been called Ruby for almost one year and seemed to like the name. Ruby became a neighborhood fixture as I grew up. Ruby was even given license to sit at my feet during classes at the Institute's Lower Form. The mantle of companion fell to Venus upon the death of her mother, Ruby. I was deeply moved by Ruby's death, was nearly inconsolable.

Venus rose to the responsibility. In fact, Venus was the one who defended me from an attack by an old boyfriend. Yes, it is ill-advised to raise your voice and your arms and hit a woman in the presence of a sixty-pound animal willing to leap on your back and sink its essentials deep into your neck when it hears a high-pitched strangled, "Stop!"

Venus had only one litter. We decided to keep a daughter from this group of puppies, Lulu. Lulu had the singular joy of growing up with two devoted mothers. Lulu was our frisky, playful, goofy baby girl. Everyday Venus, Lulu and I would go out to the park for a romp and along the streets on errands. Exercise was necessary since Lulu had a voracious appetite and was willing to eat anything that did not eat her first. Happily, Lulu loved frisbee play. We were joyous and athletic, flinging, leaping, and running, two coal-black dogs and a cinnamon-colored woman with corn-rowed hair.

Of course, Venus died. Of course, Lulu died. But Lulu gave me a puppy named Bess at the very mature age of ten years. Well, it surprised us both since Lulu had been spayed. Beautiful Bess died young, though: hit by a car on a walk. Her recently whelped puppies were bereft of their mother. I struggled to wean the puppies and put them in good homes.

From this litter came Ebony, who proved to be a simply magical dog. Ebony was Beverly's beloved mother. You remember her, M. Ebony supported and protected me throughout the difficult times with your father. Beloved Ebony. I revere her. I often think of her with great fondness.

From her came Beverly and Bev was with me when you died, M. Bless her heart, she's tried to shoulder a portion of the weight of my grief though it burdens her as well.

Love always,
Ma

June 8, 2012

Dear M.,

I have just received the following letter:

June 6, 2012

Dr. Amarantha Douglas
1352 Wintergreen Lane
Mahwah, New Jersey 10960

Dear Dr. Douglas:

I am contacting you in a state of urgency and wonder and passionate excitement. I have read your wonderful book, *Maroon New Jersey: The History of Russell's Knob, An American Town.* It has affected me deeply.

I believe myself to be descended from the people of this town. I have undertaken genealogical research through the online source, Ancestry.com and I have discovered I am a direct descendent of Bessie Stringley, a woman you mention in your book. I would like to know more about her and her family that may have come from Russell's Knob. I'm searching for information about the Stringley family. I have extensive genealogical charts. I

would be happy to bring them and confirm that I am
a direct descendent of the Stringley family. I would
like to come and access your library.

There is another compelling reason that I am
asking to visit your library and speak to you. My
family owns a bible that is stamped with the imprint
of The Langer Bible Company, Paterson, New
Jersey. You may be interested in viewing it. It is a
Family Legacy King James Bible like the ones you
mention in your book. It lists individuals I'd like
to ask you about. I would like for you to see it. It is
beautiful. Our family is Catholic.

I await your reply, Dr. Douglas. I'm very eager
to speak to you about the Bible, the Stringley
family, and Russell's Knob.

Sincerely,
Valerie O'Malley Dennis

M., talk about hot-off-the-presses. Our book was just
published in May. I've given only one talk at The Ninevah
Van Waganen House though Brynne Campbell has done
quite a bit of social media promotion. This letter surprises
me.

Love,
Ma

June 12, 2012

Dear M.,

Something in Valerie O'Malley Dennis' letter made the hairs stand at the nape of my neck. As much as she's trying to sound like an eager genealogy buff, I'm suspicious of her. She could be a journalist or some other kind of writer looking to glom onto a sexy-ish story about a White man kidnapping a free Black woman and enslaving her and taking her West and her being rescued. It's a compelling story, and I have had three inquiries about screenplay concepts.

Bessie Stringley is mentioned exactly two or three times in the entire book and only really in connection to Sheriff Emil Branch and the events connected to him. But I do know how excited a researcher can get about even one mention of a person you've been hunting for and hoping for. The question is how much she knows about the race of the Stringley family. And, aside from their connection to Emil Branch, a sheriff in Paterson who kidnapped a woman from our town and took her to the western frontier, what is there to know about the Stringley?

Well, M., of course I was titillated at the news of the family Bible. It sounds like an authentically old one of Woolman Langer's Legacy Bibles and the story of an Irish Catholic family keeping a King James Bible as a sacred artifact is intriguing. I hope it is a true story and not something this woman has fabricated as a backstory for a Bible she bought at a flea market. Even if it came from a yard sale, it could be an authentic Langer Bible. I want to see it. I've arranged to meet with her at The Ninevah Van Waganen House. She's bringing her genealogical charts and the Langer Bible. Perhaps she imagines we'll want to purchase the Bible for our collection. Maybe we will.

Ma

June 16, 2012

Yes, M., Valerie O'Malley Dennis' Bible is an authentic Langer Bible.

This from the guide to our collections, *Inside The Williams-Murtaugh Institute's Collections,* by Dr. Amarantha Douglas and Dr. Brynne Campbell:

The Family Legacy Bible Collection of Dr. Barbara Elaine Madison

Lucille Murtaugh was chief of the collecting, archiving, and preserving in the Murtaugh-Wilhelm-Smoot clan and descendants, but she was not alone. Dr Barbara Elaine Madison (1939 - 2010) was intrigued by family Bibles and collected and preserved them. The Institute's Family Legacy Bible collection is a stunning achievement.

These distinctive Bibles were kept in the homes of nearly every resident of Russell's Knob from 1870 through to the later part of the twentieth century when they were brought together in the collection oof The Williams-Murtaugh Institute. Most can be traced to 1870. The oxblood leather covers of the Langer Bibles, printed and sold by The Langer Bible Co., 144 Market Street, Paterson, New Jersey, have faded over the years so that they are various shades.

These bibles are testament to the attention that all the residents of Russell's Knob gave to their family lineages. Under the influence of Reverend Woolman Langer, a charismatic and handsome preacher who came to Paterson in 1870 at the age of sixteen, a tradition of recording family histories took root in the town after the Civil War.

Woolman Langer was ten years old when he left his enslavement on a Virginia plantation liberated by the Union Army. Woolman wandered the countryside with his mother and the two lived hand to mouth for several years until his mother's death from influenza in 1867. Langer and his mother had been enslaved to a prominent Virginia family with ties to James Madison and they had both acquired rudimentary knowledge of reading and writing. Determined to educate himself, Langer matriculated at the Philadelphia Bible College.

M., Woolman Langer's style of preaching was electric by all accounts. Here Lucille Murtaugh describes him and his sermons in some detail, especially his appearance:

Woolman Langer was the most handsome man I have ever seen. To find a fault with his face you would need to isolate each feature and critique it on its own. The larger part of Langer's beauty was in the harmonious arrangement of his features. A woman's eye had great difficulty leaving his face. His nose would have disturbed the symmetry of his face had it been one tiny bit longer or rounder or sharper. There it sat so perfectly formed between his dark ebony eyes and at watch over his gracefully plump lips. He is delightfully what we in Russell's Knob refer to as biscuit colored. He is the tan son of a tan mother. His hair, parted over his right eye, is softly kinky and always appears to have been brushed tame and shiny. He embellishes his very desirable facial features by dressing scrupulously. He has a cultured though friendly manner. He is liked equally by men and women.

Langer became a popular guest preacher in Paterson at several of the Negro congregations attended by people from Russell's Knob. Though the Smoots and Wilhelms didn't attend church services or have any interest in the Protestant Church organizations, other folks from the town began to join congregations after the Civil War. In the fall of 1870, after the harvest and the tucking in against winter had begun, Woolman Langer was invited to conduct a religious revival at the home of the VanWaganens in Russell's Knob. The then nineteen-year-old preacher-boy was magnificent according to all that was written.

Apparently, he sold a great many of the oxblood leather Bibles with his stamp on them. Based on the publication dates, Dr. Madison constructed a timeline of the wonderful preacher-boy's ministry and his introduction to and courtship of Sara Jane Smoot, who was likely one of the people who saw him at his annual revival meetings at the VanWaganen farm. She attended the Van Waganens' social functions, as her mother, Dossie, had a business relationship with them.

By all appearances, Sara Jane Smoot and Woolman Langer had the kind of marriage that others dream of. The two were handsome separately but were divinely beautiful as a couple. The evidence is clear in the many photographs taken by Ismail Murtaugh. Woolman Langer continued as an itinerant preacher until around 1910. His wife accompanied him and sold the specially imprinted Bibles along with her signature honey. These romantic rambles around the countryside in spring and summer added greatly to the stories about the firebrand preacher and his beautiful and clever wife. Many congregations welcomed Langer's fiery, theatrical performances for their revivals.

Sara Jane Smoot and Woolman Langer married in 1882. They procured a fancy covered wagon, known then as a gypsy wagon, and they worked a preaching circuit through northwestern New Jersey and eastern Pennsylvania. Sara Jane was the business head, of course. She'd come by it from early experience helping her mother build their business in bottled honey. She sold honey from the wagon along with the Langer Bibles.

After the first several years, Langer's preaching circuit was a confirmed schedule of engagements. He was truly and sincerely captivating. His sermons, though highly dramatic, were true manifestations of his faith. Langer was no con man. He was deeply devout. Sara Jane was far cooler in her religious fervor though both were passionately devoted to each other.

The Langer Bibles are not only antique, but they are, as a collection, an important documentation of the births and deaths of our town's families. And considering how many of these books must have simply been lost or destroyed over time, it is remarkable that we have as many as we have. At the time of her death, Dr. Madison's collection contained 146 of The Family Legacy King James Version of the Holy Bible, published by The Langer Bible Company, Paterson, New Jersey. I hope I can add another.

There are other bibles and sacred books with genealogical notations in The Williams-Murtaugh Institute's sacred books collection. There is the Smoot family's Bible that is older than the Langer Bibles and is one of the most valuable of Dr. Madison's collection. This book is, in fact, not a bible but a Catholic prayer book. The most historically significant of the bibles is Ernst Wilhelm/Ernest Brown's personal bible, inherited upon his death by Greta Analiese Brown and given by her to Lucille Murtaugh around the time Gree-Gree began her comprehensive history of Russell's Knob. As you may recall, Ernst Wilhelm is Petrus' father who later changed his name to Ernest Brown when he went to Canada and married his mistress, Arminty. Greta Analiese Brown is the daughter of Ernest and Arminty. The Bible is an antique German language family Bible with a print date of 1765. The print town is Nuremberg. Imagine! There is wear to the leather cover; the inner pages have yellowed; there is foxing throughout and damage to the last few pages. For a well-used book, it is in a fair condition overall.

M., I suppose it can be said that I have a strange relationship with the artifacts of The Williams-Murtaugh Institute's museum collection. I love these things though I hate some of the things they represent. I think of them as my personal legacy, my things. I think of them as literal bits of my mother and the other women in the line.

In truth, many of the Bibles came from flea markets and thrift stores. Dr. Madison was known to be a Bible collector so she would get calls. And she scoured yard sales all over New Jersey and Pennsylvania. They drew her. These Bibles have an aura about them as if they are protected by invisible powerful forces. They've survived fires and floods and insects, literally. The impermanence of paper? Hunh, I think the secret of these survivors is that they were thought to be fragile, were put in drawers for safe keeping, have a high rag content, were sometimes stored with cedar chips, and were only used to record the lineages of our town's people. This appears to have superseded their function as a reader's Bible. They were, in most cases, not daily thumbed. Consulted perhaps every birth or so. Some sat high on a shelf vulnerable to the morning sun and faded over time, their colors so various. Sometimes in the room where they now rest, Dr. Madison's library, they seem to hum and throb and ululate when one sits in there in the evening with only candles lit sipping a glass of wine.

Though Ernst Wilhelm was, like his son Petrus, something of a reprobate, he was known to read his bible on most evenings. Perhaps he used it to keep up with his German language. In 1908 when Lucille Murtaugh came into possession of the Bible twenty-eight years after the death of Ernst Wilhelm, she made the big discovery. His Bible held three crucial documents slipped in between its pages. The one most important document is the bill of sale for Lucille Murtaugh's mother, Harriet Smoot Wilhelm Murtaugh. Can you believe this paper still exists? It is a pernicious paper. It radiates bad karma It could have been destroyed many times. He didn't throw it away or burn it? He tucked it into his Bible? Did he use it to threaten and humiliate his wife? I am happy to close it up in Lucite. But it attests to something that some people would like to forget about altogether and I won't allow that. It's existence proves it all. That paper ain't no fiction.

You know that Gree-Gree's mother was sold south as a young girl and that Ernst Wilhelm bought her, married her, and brought her back to her family. He later used the same bill of sale to liberate his pregnant mistress from a bounty hunter. He was quite a character.

Also in the Bible was the letter he received from his son, Petrus Wilhelm that announces his discovery of his falsified birth certificate and Petrus' intention to join the USCT. In a cruel twist, he also placed the marriage certificate between himself as Ernest Brown and his second wife, Arminty, in this bible. This caused Arminty Brown problems after his death since she couldn't prove she had a legal marriage and was entitled to his estate. A Colored woman was never going to get title to a White man's estate without a fight, and she had no ammunition. The proof was not revealed until 1908. Who knows if Analiese Brown who came into possession of the Bible and all it contained in about 1880 as her inheritance, knew what was in the pages? Analiese and her mother did not have a constructive relationship. Analiese was treated cruelly by her mother.

It feels wrong to be excited about that paper — the bill of sale. It is an important document of witness though. We can link it to actual historical people, and we can ask museum visitors to see Harriet Smoot Wilhelm Murtaugh in her second husband's photographs at the dawn of photography and know the facts of the frightening story of her young adulthood in the nineteenth century.

It is Lucille Murtaugh who starts all of this. She is the diarist who stood at the top of the twentieth century and reached out to the twenty-first century, gathering up all that had come from the nineteenth century of our family. I've always imagined that she's reaching out to me directly. I think everyone who has ever read her diaries would say the same.

I imagine that when Lucille discovers the bill of sale, eight years after her beloved mother's death it must have been excruciatingly painful to read. And then Petrus Wilhelm would have filled in the part of the story that the paper had had in the ruse for getting Arminty out of jail and over the border to Canada. This is all covered in Lucille's account in her history of Russell's Knob. She finds out this aspect of the history when she shows the document to Petrus Wilhelm in 1908. This is the galvanizing moment for her historical research.

Dearest M., I consider those who endured the torture, the cruelty of enslavement to be the heroic ones of my line. I couldn't care less about some connection to Ernst Wilhelm's European blood. Who had the wealth means little to me. I revere the ones who struggled to make freedom for me. The one time I noticed a flair of anger at me from Brynne Campbell was when I made light jibes at the Smoots' and Wilhelms' fierce defense of their pocketbooks. She snapped at me saying that it was a privilege and a luxury not to worry about food or shelter or getting an education and that the Smoots and Wilhelms had made a comfortable life for me with their fierce acquisitiveness.

Yes, and that is what I revere about them, not their wealth. She and I agree on this point, but I think she felt she had to make the point vehemently that I mustn't take the money for granted. Yes, Ernst Wilhelm's money is at the root of it all for my family. It was his money that started his beer business and his money that purchased Harriet Smoot and returned her to her family. This money, filtered through Petrus Wilhelm's schemes and enterprises endowed the Institute. The Smoots and the Wilhelms and later the Murtaughs were what might be described today as survivalists. In the eighteenth, nineteenth, and early twentieth centuries they grew, processed, and built most of what they needed. They farmed, hunted, fished, and traded. They lived outside of the so-called White towns. They were secretive, scheming, and acquisitive. They accumulated money but didn't depend on it for survival. They survived on industry, a privilege largely unavailable to descendants.

There is a Bible that is missing from our collection. Dr. Madison searched high and low for many years in pursuit of a Bible belonging to Lucille Murtaugh herself. It has always been believed to have existed. In fact, we know from a diary entry in 1888 that Harriet Smoot Wilhelm Murtaugh gave her daughter a new deluxe edition of the Langer Bible as she left to begin study at Oberlin college. Lucille describes it in detail, "three rose-colored satin ribbons to mark its pages, a supple leather binding the color of cinnamon." She must have kept it with her. I wonder if Mary Wilhelm was also given a Langer Bible as a gift when she left for Oberlin? If so, it has not turned up either. Now that I know more of what happened to Mary, I'd like to understand more. We should scour flea markets in Ohio.

I suspect that Pearl Miller Murtaugh was unable to save those two Bibles from Robert. I suspect he destroyed his mother's Bible to keep mum the secret of his parents' identities. I find it hard not to be angry with Robert Murtaugh.

Love,
Ma

June 17, 2012

Well, M.,

Valerie O'Malley Dennis' Bible is an authentic Langer Bible. It is identical to others that we have. Valerie O'Malley Dennis arrived yesterday with perspiration on her forehead and spoke in an unbroken stream for several minutes before allowing me to offer her a seat, a cup of coffee, a place to hang her coat. When she paused with an intake of breath, I gestured to a chair and powered up the coffeemaker. She relaxed finally and ended up repeating the things she'd said upon entering my office in The Ninevah Van Waganen House.

We didn't get off to a good start. I was annoyed with Valerie for her boisterous way of entering the room. I wondered if she was always like this. Annoying. One doesn't have to be humble, but you don't have to be so loud and furiously talkative. And right away I could see she has the annoying habit of stepping on a person's answers with her next question that might be unnecessary if only she listened to the person's full answer.

Beverly reacted to my voice, my demeanor with Valerie. She raised her head at the sound of annoyance and looked at me to take the temperature of the exchange. A friendly, mellow dog, Beverly wanted me to know that she was ready to circle the wagons and send Valerie O'Malley Dennis back to her car on the run. The woman talked incessantly, and her furious barrage of words had set my teeth on edge. Responding to my mounting irritation, Beverly started to rise to her feet and take a defensive stance. I halted her with a gesture of my hand, and she relaxed. Though she would gladly lay down her life to save mine, she was relieved that she didn't have to do it just then. I heard great relief in the way she huffed and snorted as she slumped back to the floor, her stiff hips betraying her.

Then Valerie O'Malley Dennis brought the Bible out of a tote bag with a public radio logo, carelessly, clumsily, holding it with one hand only. I was appalled at the way she handled the Bible. I told her to lay it on the desk. Thinking of the way Dr. Madison handled her collection, I pulled on some gloves and a face mask and offered the woman a mask as well. I began to think of Valerie O'Malley Dennis' Bible as a poor, abused, orphan needing a home. This was dangerous because I didn't want to "fall for the book." It could be a fake. It needed to be officially authenticated though I'd authenticated it by eyeball.

I turned to the legacy page of the Bible to read the list of names. It was not so simple as one may think. The Bible was purchased or received by Elizabeth "Bessie" Stringley Branch in the 1870's. She was living in Paterson at the time. Did she come back to Russell's Knob for a revival at the Van Waganen place? Did she purchase the Bible in Paterson? What I do know is that she recorded the names and births of Stringley family members who had lived prior to the 1870's. In fact, she records several generations prior to her own in a careful hand. There is consistency to the handwriting and ink in the earliest portion as though these entries were made at the same time. The record seems to shed light on a split between Bessie Stringley's siblings and the division of their family along lines of color.

The tradition of "back-listing" individuals is common to these Bibles. They were manufactured in the 1870's, but many new purchasers noted births and identities prior to this date. They likely imported the records from other Bibles or put down what they remembered.

I hope I can help Valerie understand that the Stringleys divided not between those who were white and those who were black. They were all both black and white for several generations. That did not change. They divided because of appearance and status in the larger society. The White-looking ones moved to Paterson, got jobs that their darker relatives could not, intermarried with other ethnicities, and passed into White society.

After I closed the Bible, I felt nearly overcome with emotion. I imagined that Dr. B.E. Madison was there with her gloved hands and careful, compassionate demeanor. I wished I could feel her arms around my shoulders, standing over me peering at the Bible.

"What facts are you trying to verify, Mrs. Dennis? What do you want to know? You seem to have all the facts," I asked.

"I'm sorry?" she replied.

Yes, I had read the initial entry. Yes, I was aware of the words, and I suppose I also understood that Valerie O'Malley Dennis had come to verify her hypothesis about the Stringleys.

Of course, she wanted me to confirm that Noah and Eva, the parents of Martha Bledsoe, were enslaved on the Bledsoe Plantation. Based on what's written in the Bible, they were enslaved people of African descent who made their escape and came to settle in Russell's Knob.

"Came away." You can interpret that for yourself," I said. I realized I was speaking sharply but couldn't temper myself. Did she want me to anoint her a member of our race? Why was I so angry with this woman? Most of the people who came to Russell's Knob had come away from enslavement. "'Came away' most likely means they self-emancipated, they escaped," I softened.

Her expression changed. "Yes," she said emphatically.

Much love,
Ma

June 20, 2012

Dear M.,

Except for the Bibles, most of the information and artifacts that The Institute has pertain to the Smoot, Wilhelm, Beaulieu, and Murtaugh families. The Stringleys were not directly related to these families except that they were residents in Russell's Knob, except for the kidnapping incident. What do you know about Emil Branch? You no doubt know all. How does it work there? Are people like Branch in the same realm as you are?

He was a sheriff in Paterson just prior to the Civil War. He's the brother of Valerie O'Malley Dennis' ancestor Olive, who was the daughter of Bessie Stringley Branch. Olive Branch. I wonder why they named her that? Emil Branch had three children. Olive lists their births. I told Valerie he was the kidnapper; he was known to have been the abductor. He became obsessed with Dossie Smoot, a young matron at the time. He had a grudge against the Smoot family and was known to have used his authority to menace women.

"My goodness." Valerie said, when I explained her family tree contained an abductor. She opened her mouth to say something more, but closed it, opening and closing it several more times. She expected to be shocked but was expecting that the shock would be that I confirmed some of the Stringley family had been enslaved.

"Enslaved." I prefer to say that people were enslaved. That puts the onus on the one who did the enslaving. No one is born a slave. They are enslaved. Tortured.

Ma

June 25, 2012

Dear M.,

Valerie returned yesterday. We met again in the Ninevah. I prepared a fact sheet of the information I've researched.

Facts about the Stringley Family of Russell's Knob, New Jersey

Bessie Stringley was the oldest girl of Eben Stringley and Martha Bledsoe. Her younger sisters were Harriet and Martha. Her brothers, older and younger, were Nathaniel, Numa, William, and James. Though she obviously purchased the Bible no earlier than 1870, Bessie Stringley lists the names of some of her grandparents. No dates. Bessie Stringley writes that Martha Bledsoe's parents came away from the Eastern Shore. "Noah and Eva came away from Bledsoe" is what she writes, is how she begins as if defying contradiction or erasure. It appears that Bessie Stringley, having left her past, her history, and her race behind when she crossed over Paterson's color line to marry a White man, still wanted to preserve a truthful part of her history, a true person of Russell's Knob. It can be seen as a practical step to ensure a certain future that she married a White man in the town of Paterson. But she could have married a White-looking man in Russell's Knob so I figured she must have wanted a fully White, privileged life.

Bessie Stringley married William Branch in 1841. Harriet and Martha, similarly White-skinned as their sister, also married men in Paterson who were considered White. Harriet Stringley married Antonio Marianni and Martha Stringley married Alexander Odabashian, an Armenian fruit merchant. Nathanial, Numa, William, and James Stringley remained in Russell's Knob, married local women, and continued to live as mixed-race people. People in Russell's Knob did not live as Black people or White people. They simply lived as themselves.

What is meant is that there were no places that a Black person in our town could not be, things they could not do. People were, first and foremost, clannish. They clung to their extended family which, by and large, was most of the other people in town. They were fiercely loyal to their family and clan and town. So the Stringley clan in Russell's Knob appears to have flourished. Even the unsettling incident of the Dossie Smoot kidnaping by Emil Branch did not ostracize the entire family. Throughout her life, Bessie Stringley apparently kept up with all her family members. She lists her siblings' children in the bible, on both sides of the color line.

M., I've decided that I'd like to have this book for our collection. There is something unique about this record, something very Russell's Knob-ish. The disinclination, the inability to leave anyone out no matter who they are or were.

Ma

June 30, 2012

Dear M.,

Now that Dr. Campbell has studied the cemetery records in fine detail, a picture is emerging. We now think we know what happened to Emil Branch. He became obsessed with Dossie Smoot. Branch menaced her in Paterson, where she and her sister-in-law operated a vegetable and honey stand. She resisted, and he raped her. The most likely consequence of this is that Branch was killed in retribution by some of the Smoot and Wilhelm men. Their idea of self-defense was a healthy dose of vengeful acts visited on any outside enemy.

According to the secret ledger, Branch is buried in the Old Smoot/Russell's Knob Cemetery, his body hidden in a family grave. This is the fate of many men who came to Russell's Knob tracking and hunting the self-emancipated people who took refuge there. Martha Bledsoe's parents likely arrived here, too, with their hearts in their mouths pursued by someone.

It is disturbing, but there is a ledger. Duncan Smoot dictated information to his daughter days before his death. Apparently, he'd kept a mental record of the internments that he and his father and his nephews were responsible for. I'm not sure why. I suppose one is haunted by opening a relative's grave and heaving in the body of somebody else. Why set down this horrifying information? To keep straight the ghosts? Who knows why? Sara Jane Smoot recorded the information her father gave her in a record book and put it alongside the Smoot Bible. Believe it not, no one had read it until Dr. Campbell examined it.

It lists an "E.B., sheriff in Paterson." I knew what it meant immediately. It meant that the whole story of the abduction was fabricated to cover up something more local and dangerous, the killing of a White sheriff from Paterson. This is the more plausible scenario.

M., Emil Branch left a lot of carnage in his family in Paterson, too.

According to what facts Valerie O'Malley Dennis has, he just vanished without a word. He drained all his money from the bank and took off. His wife had to go to work in the factory, lost an arm in an accident, and drank up her settlement money. The two sons and a daughter went to work in the factory, too. Bessie must have lost track of them because she recorded no descendants for them. Valerie's descended directly from Emil's younger sister, Olive. With that name, she must have been a charmer. She married into a huge Irish Catholic family, the O'Malleys. She must have clung to the Bible for a sense of herself as her mother had done. Her O'Malley sons filled it to the brim with their progeny.

Yes, M., despite myself, I like that fulsomeness. Clearly Olive Branch just wanted to keep hold of something that her mother had honored and prized and then had replicated this feeling and passed it to her generations. I can't help but feel that this is down to Russell's Knob, the kind of place it was. What does it mean to be descended from these people, these recorders, these survivors? Whether or not they were ever aware of their roots in Russell's Knob, the Branches, the O'Malley, the Mariannis, and the Odabashians have a glimmer of those old souls in their genes. I've arranged to have Valerie's family history added to our archives.

I confirmed the basic information about Emil Branch to Valerie. He was like most men of his day. A woman's body was a possession. He took what he wanted when he raped Dossie Smoot, and the Smoot and Wilhelm men made him pay, acting out their privilege as men to assert their prior ownership. Frankly, the ignominious burial in a group grave, is disgusting, too. I'm descended from the Smoots, and it does not make me especially proud that they chose this solution to dispose of their enemies. That's the problem with genealogical research and digging into the past. There is real ugliness. Malefactors have families, too. And Emil left a scar on the Branch family. If he hadn't been such a pig, if our society did not give him absolute authority to do these things, the women of both families would not have suffered.

I know Valerie can't quite see it from my point of view. I feel this White man, being a sheriff and all, had his good reputation all these decades though he was a brutal, bestial person who preyed on women, Black women. They suffered. Their families suffered. He got his comeuppance. But because all this vengeance was done in secret, he kept his good name in the Branch family. It's what we harp on as privilege. The Branch family had the Whiteness, the thing they awarded themselves, a thing for which Bessie Stringley and her sisters left their family hearth. Assumptions are made about people who are White and, in the days we're speaking about here, great latitude was given for certain things that would be considered egregious today. Like rape. I'm not sorry they killed Emil Branch.

Valerie and I agreed about that. I urged her not to abandon the Bible because of him. Sweet little Olive Branch is in there with all her big, pale, light-haired sons. According to the Bible, she had eight of them. Valerie brought the photograph of Olive and her sons. A tiny old lady in a black dress is surrounded by eight tall men. It was taken at her husband's funeral in 1915.

And the cryptic information about Bledsoe is recorded in that Bible. M., I guess we ought to know about Bledsoe. It is why Bessie Stringley set all that genealogical information down I suppose. She wanted us to understand some vital thing about her. Valerie and I have agreed to find out about Bledsoe together.

Love,
Ma

July 5, 2012

Dear M.,

"What to the slave is your fourth of July?" – Frederick Douglass

You know I steadfastly refuse to celebrate the so-called Independence Day. What a crock!

What is there to know about Bledsoe? I've decided to find out about The Stringleys first. Brynne Campbell is looking at the Bible. She was very excited. I'm delighted at her enthusiasm for The People. She's embraced them as her family, and I'm pleased. It's very like The People to take in someone who wants a refuge.

She'll be adding the listings of individuals to her database of the town's inhabitants, its people. Valerie O'Malley Dennis' people now, too. Valerie beamed tomato red when I told her. She has that easily flushed, pale complexion, and I was reminded that Gree-Gree said Petrus Wilhelm did also. We looked at photographs, what ones I could lay my hands on quickly, of the Stringley family.

We have found a very small town on the Eastern Shore called Bledsoe, a plantation owned and operated by Pecival Bledsoe. Is this the "Bledsoe" that Noah and Eva came away from?

M., I've always believed that Lucille's gentle presentiment of the future is written especially for me. I am the generations she speaks of, and I have come into possession of her diaries, her papers, her things. The responsibility is huge. Ah! What has happened to you, makes it even more urgent, doesn't it?

Your Ma

August 5, 2012

Dearest M.,

This past month has been the saddest time I have passed through since I lost you, my sunshine. My other sun has left me. My beloved Beverly has gone. Listen to me. Trying to sound so pitiful as if the animal wanted to leave me, wanted to die. No, like every dog I have ever known and loved, she clung to me until her common sense as an animal told her it was time to go. Of course, she turned that face up to me and I had to do the horrible, unthinkable, but humane thing. I wished I was a dog then. I wish I was able to put my comings and goings in someone else's hands. What might I have done differently? Dogs never die in their sleep, dammit. For a week, I hoped each night that she would die in her sleep and save me from having to put her down. I hoped Beverly would, but I haven't had a dog yet who did. This was the biggest test of my courage that I can recollect. I say this because, when you died, other people did the heavy lifting on my behalf. I was devastated. I could not act.

Valerie O'Malley Dennis went with me to the vet with Beverly if you can believe that. Sometimes you just have to let people help you. She insisted and we went to a diner for lunch after.

Valerie and I have been working closely researching Bledsoe Plantation and its connection to her ancestors. I suppose we are growing on each other. I remember how wary Beverly was of her on that first afternoon we met.

The aromas of those things I usually don't notice rise to my nose when I put on the mindfulness tapes and sit thinking of Beverly. These, I know, are the small scents she smelled always. These were her markers, her clues, fresh mown grass two doors down from Mrs. Simpson up early and busy about her yard, the lingering scent of perfume on yesterday's t-shirt that I wore to the drugstore on top of my everyday jeans that I feel free to be gassy in. Bev and I were soul sisters.

I grew up with dogs and have always been careless with crumbs as a result. Dogs are greedy animals. They love to scoop up anything you've left. I'm always aware of this when I'm in a hotel and I am careless of crumbs. I miss Beverly especially and sorely at these times, at breakfast, at lunch and at dinner, morning, noon, and night. Ah! A happy thought! Bev is with you surely. You are patting her head even now. I suppose they all are there with you. How does it work?

Come to me in a dream, Malcolm,
Ma

August 15, 2012

Dear M.,

Mr. Lenny read me like a book the last time I went to see him. We ate ham sandwiches and talked about the way winter was different now and how summer had changed, too. Climate change. *Something* changed, Mr. Lenny said. We talked about Beverly. How it is so painful to let a pet go home to its glory, but too painful to watch them suffer. We had a taste of whiskey. Oh, how I miss Beverly and you! I think there is a dangerous tipping point in this life. When your loved ones have all crossed, you can get very gloomy and wistful, lax about clinging to your own life. I think Mr. Lenny heard this in my voice.

A sound is missing from my life. The sound of several metal tags tinkling against a leather collar, scraping the floor. This sound attached to the neck of someone who noted my comings and goings, always attending to my rising and moving about. I miss this sorely.

I went over to Mr. Lenny's niece, Rebecca's house to see her new puppies, M. Why not? She had called to say her dog had puppies, beautiful ones, did I want one. She said she'd heard about Beverly. Well, there is no set time to mourn for a dog. It isn't about mourning really. It's knowing when you're ready for the commitment again. Wow, a puppy, a baby animal, a heartbeat wrapped in fur with a warm stomach, a nose like a leather purse and two dark, soulful eyes. Why not go to the animal shelter to get a dog? Because I'm going to pick out a puppy from a lovingly chaotic household full of children and dogs and a couple of cats and Rebecca's cheerful outlook. The puppy needs a forever home in a house with no children, but with vet appointments and undivided attention. The litter has four boys and four girls. Labs like to deliver up a nice big bunch equally divided by gender. Rebecca's dog Precious is a black Labrador retriever and the puppies' father is one of two brown scalawags in the neighborhood. Half of the puppies are blackish-brown, and half are coal black. All of them have brown points above their eyes so I'm guessing the father is Rebecca's neighbor's Rottweiler. Phew! She'll become a very large dog. Taking a puppy is always taking a chance on an individual. Each dog is an individual who transcends breed specific traits. So, some part of the pact is taking a chance on yourself. You're entering a relationship, a deep commitment to honesty and constancy from cradle to grave through rain and snow and dark of night. Am I up for it? I want this, but am I capable of the care? Can I mold this individual into a good companion? If this puppy turns out to be mostly a Rottweiler, then I'll be picking up turds the size of a loaf of bread. Am I down for that?

M., of course, I'm going to adopt one of these furry stalwarts. I am going to revel in the aroma of her and not think about the size of shit. I've been testing myself the past few weeks. Yes, I'm ready. I've chosen one of the females from Precious' litter. I'm allowing my heart out for a spin again. She is coal black with the same brown points as her siblings.

Taking care of the dog will keep me to a schedule, give me a framework for my day. I realize I've missed so much since Beverly's been gone. Without Beverly I haven't kept to my exercise, rambling around the neighborhood on our walks. There are people I haven't spoken to in weeks. I don't know their names. We encountered them on walks. They'd see Beverly's beautiful black, velvet snout and magnificently lustrous Labrador Retriever coat and understand that I was a good and caring person. If your dog's coat shines like a pair of patent leather pumps at Easter, then you are a good person.

Remember? We came to be viewed as harmless Blacks, the college professor, her son, and the gentle, friendly dog. Remember there were people who only spoke to us when we walked with Beverly? Well, the neighborhood hasn't changed much since you died. Which also means that there are people, White people, who look at me longer than they look at any other person. A few of the more recent arrivals appear surprised to see me getting in and out of the car in the driveway carrying bags of groceries. They haven't seen me ambling through the neighborhood with a dog. They think I'm the housekeeper. They wonder if I belong here, they wonder how many like me there are in their new neighborhood. I need a dog for their sakes. Hah! They'll think I'm a dog walker.

Perhaps canines' keenest accomplishment is that they get along with humans and thrive in the relationship. Perhaps also we imagine that when they look at us they will judge us if we are not honest, or brave or, at least intelligent. That knowing look is influential, but they really are not judgmental. They'll lick your hand even if you have throttled your mother. Maybe not. Maybe they draw the line at murder. Little else.

I am naming my new puppy Dorothy Throckmorton. It makes me smile to say it. It's a funny improbable name and that's part of the fun of having a new dog, isn't it? You choose the name you'd have chosen for yourself or something that makes you laugh. I'll call her Dottie because of the brown points above her eyes and because it is playful, Lottie Dottie, Polka Dottie.

It is silly to attempt to draw lines and connections between all the dogs I've had and shared with you and your grandmother, but Dorothy comes to me as an old soul in a new body. Her line of canines has been in and around the towns and homes that are where Russell's Knob used to be for generations. Surely Dottie has some part of the souls of her forebears. It is not about replacing a loved one, human, canine, whatever, with another loved one. The human emotions that we associate with pangs and twinges in our chests, call them heartstrings or whatever, need regular exercise. Neglect them at your peril. They must be stretched and kept elastic for us to thrive. Caring for a companion dog is great exercise for the muscle. This is the exercise I need. I'm fine by myself, but I'm better when someone needs me.

I have sorely needed you, my love.

Love,
Your Ma

September 4, 2012

Dear M.,

Dorothy seems to believe that my feet are my most important appendage. She settles on top of them whenever I sit. And, despite the really plush (looks comfortable to me) dog bed I bought, she sleeps on the floor, on a rag rug, with her face shoved into one of my slippers and her little body stretched on top of the other slipper. She wants to know me. Unencumbered by propriety, she's studying me in her doggie sleep, inhaling all my secrets through the fumes my feet leave in those slippers. That's a dog's work for you, extracting someone's soul through the soles of their feet and getting the truth out of the places we're always trying to hide, cover, or mitigate the stink of. Who we are is essentially what we eat and where we go. Dogs understand this.

M., people in the old place, in Russell's Knob in its heyday, used to eat squirrel regularly. Young children in the town set dogs on them and targeted them with slingshots, BB guns, and rifles. So, we were a people who ate squirrels well into the twentieth century because they were numerous when chickens and cows and pigs were not, and we came to like the taste of them. I have noticed that this young dog hates squirrels, acts like we ought to hunt them together. I'd never touch squirrel stew unless my life depended on it. And Dr. Barbara Elaine Madison, ensconced on her heavenly throne, raises her index finger, and waggles it at me. "Girl, you don't know what you might have to do some day," she'd say. I tell Dorothy to forget squirrels. We'll catch, skin, and roast our food at the Stop & Shop. She knows this, too. Canine anamnesis gives her a wide spectrum of knowledge: the past, the present and the afterlife.

Love,
Ma

September 15, 2012

Dear M.,

Well, I had to pick my jaw up off the floor. Brynne Campbell announced her pregnancy today. I had no idea that she had made this plan. I understood she was a lesbian. I thought that precluded any interest in having a baby. I'm afraid I had a real lack of imagination. Of course, a person as smart and dedicated as Brynne Campbell would want to be a mother and will be an exemplary mother. I hadn't noticed the outward signs. What is wrong with me? I'm ashamed to think I hadn't even paid close attention to her. She explained that she didn't tell me because she didn't want to be dissuaded by me or even influenced much. She said that, because of her bad parenting experience, she decided to undergo invitro and raise her child as a single parent all by herself, on her own terms.

I'm surprised. This shows just how conventional I am. I'm surprised at her choice and surprised at myself for being so uncreative. Finally, I hugged her and could feel the slight bulge in her abdomen. How could I have missed this? Oh, well, we don't often see what we're not looking for.

She has come along four and a half months and wants me to come along on her ultrasound. Wow. I haven't been part of anything like this in a long time.

Love,
Ma

November 2, 2012

Dear M.,

I've hunted through the Bibles in Dr. Madison's collection to find the one with our details, the records of the Smoot descended. I've decided to put our Hope (this is the name Brynne's chosen) in it. In fact, it didn't take long to find. Our family details were in the Smoot Family Bible, which served as record of our family people since before Gree-Gree's day. In fact, this Bible was just a book for recording births and deaths according to anecdotal evidence. Its pages were rarely turned. I'm ordering a Mont Blanc pen to record the birth. I'm so happy, so expectant, so ready for this bliss.

Brynne described her childhood as having been mis-parented, mishandled, misused. She came up in the foster system. By her account she was given nothing but pain and fear and uncertainty by people who never felt the overwhelming joy in parenting that she feels now. She has paid me the compliment of asking if I will be her parenting mentor. Of course, of course.

Love,
Ma

February 25, 2013

Dear M.,

I say to you, from the depths of grief and confusion, there is no God or god or good or any other bullshit, omniscient presence to whom to appeal. How could the sincere and sacred longing to bring a healthy and beloved child into the world, that longing not be granted purchase? No prayers needed. Believers have an answer, but I don't buy them. I say to myself that I will never smile again on this earth. Because the baby didn't die so somebody has got to smile to welcome her on this side. But how can I be that somebody that smiles? I feel like I've got a leaden blanket on my chest like the ones put on for x-rays at the dentist.

The last six months of Brynne's pregnancy were calm though she was excited in ways that she'd never experienced before. She was in a whirlwind of preparation. I hadn't remembered so much planning and readying.

You are omniscient. I am not. I tell you what has happened though you must surely know already. Maybe you saw it coming but had no way to warn us. Mine is a response. I am telling something back to myself. I know what has happened, or think I do. You know everything. What in the name of hell happened? And what in the name of hell have I undertaken?

M., hold her hand. Meet her at the gate. Is there a gate, a

door? My imaginings are limited. Whatever is the threshold, help her through, Beloved.

I tell you that Brynne Campbell was brilliant and good. How am I going to look in that baby's face and not see her brilliance and beauty and not want to wail at the injustice of Brynne's death caused by this child's life? Yet, there in that face will always be Brynne's intellect. For no other reason, I must stay alive and thrive.

Hope was born on February 19, 2013. Brynne died on February 20, 2013. I feel very much alone except that this tiny child has a hold on me. I've got to step up to care for her.

Help me,
Ma

September 10, 2013

My dearest Malcolm,

How I wish you could be here for this occasion. There have been many days I've wanted to have you physically by my side. Today is the ultimate.

I've been given Hope, capital H and little h. I keep pondering and pondering it, and I get a delighted feeling coursing all through my body. I have not felt this way in a very long time, since you were born. I wish I could see you here today in a tux. You were my life's best goal. I not only suffered the loss of you, your body, but the loss of all my dreams and goals for you. It has been crushingly painful without you. But today is a joyous day. I've been pronounced fit and proper and legally mandated to care for Hope, big and little. I am bathed in delight. I am suffused with joy. I dressed up for the occasion. But, at the same time, I am rubbed raw with sadness.

You have met Brynne by this time. My goodness, how much of this can I take! I can, and will, take it all now. If it were not for Hope, I'd be ready to check myself out of this life. For real. I mean, can I survive much more grief? But this time, unbelievably, incomprehensibly, I can't do that. I really can't check out. And I am now too superstitious to even consider that there is no grief left on my account. I could be bereft again.

I am so angry, beyond mere anger. I am enraged, fully engorged with rage at times. But the imperative to care for baby Hope is keeping me moderately calm. How could her mother have died this way? Her obstetrician pretends to be puzzled, has said that Brynne suddenly went sour. What does that even mean? There was not a sour muscle in Brynne Campbell's whole body. She appeared healthy. I know she was happy, was exhilarated to be bringing Hope into the world. She had settled everything in her head and in her life. She knew she wanted to raise her child as a single mother. She'd already started a college account and bought a car seat and a breast pump and thought that she could certainly home school.

I told her that whenever she needed me, I'd be there. She consulted a lawyer and drew up a guardianship agreement for me to sign. I told her I would always love and care for her child. She left nothing undone that I can see. She took care of everything on Hope's behalf. I wonder if she had some kind of presentiment of this horrible circumstance. The doctor said her blood pressure spiked precipitously, and she suffered a series of strokes the day after Hope was born. Brynne had held her, had kissed her. Oh, my goodness! Sudden death is the only kind of death I know.

I have something to tell Brynne and you must deliver it to her in your capacity as medium. Give her my pledge that Hope will grow and thrive.

When I began this conversation with you ,I was missing you so terribly and missing Mother recently deceased, and it made me anxious to fill up the time, to hear another voice even if it was but an echo of my own. I needed that for a long time. Even then I wasn't a hermit. I had a social life that was mostly fundraising dinners and birthday check-ins. But I was overwhelmed with loneliness. It was physical. I felt like I was standing in a furious headwind and that I would topple and blow away. I felt a burning urge to tell somebody all my personal anecdotes, the stories I'd saved up for you. I wanted to discuss my keen insights on our peoples' history, wanted to chart the course of my sorrows at being left here in this life without you and Mother. Have I interrupted your life among the stars, in the heavenly place I imagine where you dwell with Mother and Gree-Gree, and all the others? Sorry.

I have Hope now but you are not, however, off the hook for the rest of my earthly existence. You are not relieved of my need for you. Please don't think that I won't want you near now that I have Hope. Please understand that I think little Hope has lifted my maternal spirits to a point where they are useful and productive again. I feel alive. When the anniversary of your death came, for the first time I forgot the day's significance until the worst, the early morning, of it was over. This is a positive, necessary step. I recognize that. Some things should be forgotten. Not you, but that day above all.

I still count on your heavenly agency. I have reckoned on it quite a bit these many years. I will always believe that your death was untimely, a tragic accident out of sync with the universe's plans. I was left dangling. I have held on only because I held onto the idea of you being close by. I'm sorry. Have I kept you close by because I wanted and needed you so much? Has my conjuring kept you from romping in fields of glory, from scaling mountains, from flying about? I've always thought you must have been given some magic presence, some extra-normal communication with me because your passing left me bereft. I have shamelessly felt I was owed more of you. But was it fair of me to require your vigilance in my head and on my shoulder? I have no understanding of proximity in the afterlife. I think I've likely wrung you dry with my pining and weeping and feeling aggrieved and grieving. I hope not. I hope I haven't spoiled your eternity with my clinging keeping you from a full realization of what it is that is next.

Maternal energy is our great elastic, the compelling movement back and forward between our ancestors and our descendants. We are all "born of woman to live awhile and love and die." We are all in the middle of it then, neither first nor last.

Are you relieved to be done with the appeals for magical intervention? Forget it. I see you laughing. Your face has exploded in hundreds of delightful wrinkles and crinkles and your skin has turned nearly purple. I feel your giggles and guffaws on my chest as if I'm holding onto you, and you are laughing, laughing, laughing with your body pressed against mine. I've got more now to ask for. You have a sister to look out for now. Need I remind you of what it means to your clan that you protect and honor your little sister?

Have you communed with Petrus Wilhelm and Old Duncan Smoot? Oh, I know you've encountered these old roosters. Reprobates like those two aren't necessarily in hell. Does such a place exist? I imagine rather that upon gaining the afterlife they clearly see their failings and transgressions. Their hell is their recognition and deep shame at these actions.

This realization must come to us all. Thus, their family loyalties and bravery have earned them a seat at your table. Ah! My thoughts about the afterlife are so conventional, tables and chairs and doors and coffee and wine. But surely now you have insights about a brother's duty to his mother's daughter.

Now, above all, I want to stay alive for a nice long while to look after Hope. I know you can't snatch me there, and I know you can't influence my longevity. Just forgive me for promising that I would come to be with you in a short while. When you died, I promised not to want to live long without you. I want to stay if I can now. I'm sorry I didn't know what I was talking about back then.

I'd like to be stuck here a while.

What I've wanted to accomplish in these writings addressed to you is give you the knowledge I was charged with passing to you. And now I am wishing and praying to stay alive and hearty to give the knowledge and all to Hope. Mother gave me Lucille Murtaugh's diaries to read when I was eighteen or so, before I went to college. I meant to give them to you, too. I called myself waiting a bit until I felt you'd understand them better. Forgive me for being so constrained by gendered ideas, thinking there was some mystery about being male and that you were on a mission to solve it. Feeling a bit guilty about raising you without a guiding male presence is what it mostly had to do with. I thought Gree-Gree's diaries would have more meaning for a young girl rather than a young man. I wasn't thinking clearly in those years.

My mother was more generous and trusting. She was a

questioner always, was nevertheless very attuned to ritual and observance. She wanted to mark a moment for me when she gave me the diaries to read and annotate. She said that if I was unmoved by them, it would be acceptable, but she would know what I knew about our People. I could have said that to you. Of course, I was and continue to be deeply, profoundly touched by my wonderful ancestor's journals and diaries. And, of course, I wanted you to know this valuable history, too. Was I afraid you wouldn't be as enthusiastic about them as I was? Sort of. You seemed to want to shrug me off a bit, and I understood that feeling and I wanted you to know it was alright. I didn't want to impose the diaries on you. I thought there was plenty of time. I hesitated and your fate found you in that dorm.

My goodness, Malcolm, I am sorry about the diaries. They would have been as important to you as they were to me. Would anything have been different for you if I had given them to you? If the merest thing had been the slightest bit different, slower, faster, wider, narrower, earlier, later, flammable, inflammable, hostile or not hostile, could it have changed the course of your history? If you'd been in the library reading the diaries, would you have died that day? You see where devastating, sudden bereavement can bring you, circuitous, loopy thinking. Years of "what ifs."

Except that "everything is everything" is what people say because for some reason it makes them comfortable that everything is connected in time. Perhaps it is not. Perhaps it is indeterminate and what sounds like some old foolishness turns out to be truly some old foolishness. You would know. Everything is everything because who the hell can say what everything is. Mellow thinking, baby.

Is there wine on the other side, Malcolm? Is there no need of wine, or no want of wine? I consider this. Heaven should be a very happy, happy place and wine would help with that, as well as reefer. But it might get kind of boring with everyone sitting around having wine and being a bit tipsy and could get ugly if you tried to cut people off. So, is there wine in heaven? Beer? Whiskey? Reefer?

I sincerely hope that Brynne is at glorious rest there. Despite the anguish of leaving her beloved child, I hope she is . . . I don't know what one wishes for the dead. To be at peace? Perhaps death is one long spell of rest at peace. Some people would hope it were so.

My challenge is to strike the balance between grieving Brynne properly and raising her baby. I am throwing myself in completely. Parenting this girl is the last great undertaking of my life. (I better be careful of what I say!) I've got to do it right. Brynne trusted me to fill the role. But besides that, this is my heart's imperative. M., tell he, I will take care of Hope. It is probably not at all necessary. She knows my heart.

I hope you will understand that I am breaking off our correspondence, at least for the next while. I've got my hands full, and my waking hours are well occupied. You have sustained me, M.

I love you always, Malcolm
Ma

EPILOGUE

September 15, 2020

Hope's an independent child coddled but capable. She's a competent cook. She can pull together spaghetti, meat sauce and a salad reliably. She often does. Lately though, Amy is hoping for something other than pasta on Hope's cooking nights. The pandemic and the quarantine, this frightening patch the world is experiencing, and a great many people are not surviving, has exacerbated the boredom of spaghetti and spaghetti and angel-hair spaghetti. A person can get obsessed with fixing the one thing they think they're good at. For Amy it had been fried chicken accomplished at an early age, considered an excellent and very much adult accomplishment. Yes, yes, she was good at it, but fried is not so much wanted anymore.

Playing video games, watching TikTok videos, cooking and working through assignments leaves hours to fill. Evwen though she is used to working alone on schoolwork, Hope is still restless and bored. Searching through her mother's collection of thumb drives in her desk started her work, cataloguing photographs. The instinct to collect is part of her DNA. Is there a specific gene for archiving?

Shortly before the pandemic and all the unimaginable things, wearing masks and arguing about wearing masks and not going places and not doing things and not hugging people and using hand sanitizer, Hope and her mother had begun work on "The Project." The project was assembling the coffee table book that Hope's late biological mother had conceived. Dr. Brynne Campbell had wanted to publish a book of photographs of the people of Russell's Knob. She'd conceived of it as a big, beautiful proof that this place and these people had been real.

Ismail Murtaugh's photographic plates and prints were a huge, disorganized mess of documentation and Brynne Campbell was enormously excited by them. She'd received funding to restore damaged plates and develop them. She was deep into bringing them to narrative order when she died. She had identified many people, but the work was not yet half completed. Amy knew that a day would come when she and Hope could bring the book into fruition. But grief has its own schedule, and they were only now able to begin the work. The development process was long and expensive. Now, finally, all the undamaged plates have been developed and digitized.

Since her mother tested positive for COVID-19, Hope has been head nurse and chief cook on their quarantine island. For safety's sake, Amy has closeted in her room, using her adjoining bathroom, and is giving out directives through her closed bedroom door and via video calls. A crisis like this makes her question the arrangement of raising and caring for an seven-year-old alone. It worries her because this COVID is real. That much is very clear. People have died suddenly. Have left things undone. Have gutted whole families. Black people at the top of the list.

Rebecca Vander Jackson is Hope's back-up adult. Mr. Lenny, Rebecca's uncle, was set to go to a senior facility, but with the pandemic, they aren't admitting any new patients. Rebecca's hands are full of kids and Mr. Lenny, and she's scared not to go in to take her shift at the grocery store. But looking out for the people she's supposed to look out for is in her DNA. She's been checking in with Hope and Amy each morning thanks to her son, Ponce. He set up a check-in network on Zoom. The brightest spot of the day! Everybody combing their hair and trying to smile over the video call. Hope is young, but she's a smart kid. She's been acting sunny and brave on Zoom. She knows she better act brave if she wants to stay in her house. If she acts scared, they're liable to move her in with Rebecca and leave her mother alone.

Yes, she's been using a mask when entering her mother's bedroom. Yes, she is washing dishes with lots of dish soap and very hot water and using the plastic gloves and wiping doorknobs and asking the delivery people to leave it on the mat and NOT going outside except to walk Danbury and wearing a mask and staying six feet back from everybody and taking her phone everywhere and always wearing a mask.

Rebecca tells her not to listen to TV news before sleeping. Daily reports of deaths and hospitalizations is not the stuff of dreams. Rebecca tells her not to be scared because this thing will pass over.

Hope listens to her mother breathing. She didn't tell Rebecca, but she put an old baby monitor she found in the closet in her mother's room. She listens off and on through the night. They've been watching the blood oxygen levels and Amy continues to improve. Her doctor, visibly relieved to say so via video house call, assured them that Amy

Douglas' illness is on the mild side and should be treated at home rather than the hospital. She must be quarantined in her bedroom until she can test negative, but don't bring her to the emergency room unless . . . "You'll know," she said, "Don't come unless you must."

Rebecca was right. COVID-19 was passing over and through everybody. Hope noted when her mother's breathing became quieter. At first, she'd gotten scared and crept into her mother's room to see about her, to listen to her. Amy was beathing softly and deeply not hitching and rattling. It was clear that she felt better, the illness was easing.

September 20, 2020

Dear M.,

I love you. I was scared, but now I'm not. I saw you sleeping. You look better.

I think I ought to tell what I did.

I read your letters to Malcolm. I went and loaded a thumb drive looking for more pictures for the book. I saw the special thumb drive, so I loaded it. I opened the file that had letters to Malcolm. I kept on reading because I figured you wanted me to if you crossed over and didn't come back. I know. I know a person doesn't have any control over coming and going. I know you'd stay with me no matter what, if you could. But what if you couldn't?

I'm tough, Ma. I'm like all the tough women from The People. I know where I'm going, and I know I'm going to get there.

Hope

BREENA CLARKE is the author of three novels, most recently ***Angels Make Their Hope Here***, set in an imagined mixed-race community in 19th-century New Jersey. Breena Clarke's debut novel, ***River, Cross My Heart***, was an October 1999 Oprah Book Club selection. Her critically reviewed second novel, ***Stand The Storm,*** is set in mid-19th century Washington, D.C. Her short fiction has appeared in *Kweli Journal*, The *Stonecoast Review*, NOW online magazine, *Nervous Breakdown*, *Mom/Egg review*, and *Catapult*, as well as, *Like Light: 25 Years of Poetry & Prose by Bright Hill Poets & Writers*. She has contributed to the anthology, ***IDOL TALK: Women Writers on the Teenage Infatuations That Changed Their Lives***. Breena is co-editor of ***Chicken Soup for the Soul I'M SPEAKING NOW: BLACK WOMEN SHARE THEIR TRUTHS IN 101 STORIES OF LOVE, COURAGE AND HOPE*** to which she contributed two personal narratives. Breena Clarke is co-founder and co-organizer of The Hobart Festival of Women Writers, an annual celebration of the work of women authors since 2013. She is co-editor of NOW online journal of The Hobart Festival of Women Writers

ACKNOWLEDGMENTS

A work may have one author, but it needs many supporters to become a novel. I have been fortunate to have the guidance, camaraderie, and critical eyes of my sister-writers, Cheryl Clarke, and Esther Cohen. Their advice has been invaluable. I acknowledge and appreciate Stephanie Nikolopoulos for her deft editorial assistance. I also recognize the many writers who have participated in Hobart Festival of Women Writers. Their stunning creative works and their community have inspired and encouraged me. Special thanks to Helmar Augustus Cooper.